I Can Always Sleep Tomorrow

October, 2003

Judy -
Love always,

EJ

I Can Always Sleep Tomorrow

Real Life stories of Love and Larceny, Adventure and Awakening

Everett Elting

Trafford Publishing
301 South Front Street, Suite 8
New Bern, North Carolina, 28560

Printed in Victoria, Canada

Art Direction – Peter Weis
Design – Steve Dunk, Reactor
Illustrations – Jeff Jackson

National Library of Canada Cataloguing in Publication Data

Elting, Everett, 1936-
        I can always sleep tomorrow : real-life stories of love and larceny, adventure and
awakening / Everett Elting.
ISBN 1-4120-0759-3
        I. Title.
PS8559.L83T78 2003   C813'.6   C2003-903840-8

TRAFFORD

This book was published *on-demand* in cooperation with Trafford Publishing.
On-demand publishing is a unique process and service of making a book available for retail sale to the public taking advantage of on-demand manufacturing and Internet marketing. **On-demand publishing** includes promotions, retail sales, manufacturing, order fulfilment, accounting and collecting royalties on behalf of the author.

Suite 6E, 2333 Government St., Victoria, B.C. V8T 4P4, CANADA
Phone   250-383-6864   Toll-free   1-888-232-4444 (Canada & US)
Fax   250-383-6804   E-mail   sales@trafford.com
Web site   www.trafford.com   TRAFFORD PUBLISHING IS A DIVISION OF TRAFFORD
HOLDINGS LTD.
Trafford Catalogue #03-1127   www.trafford.com/robots/03-1127.html

10   9   8   7   6   5   4   3

Contents

Dedicated to the memory of my parents, Everett and Louise.

Once, many years ago, I was trying to choose between two different desired activities. I went to mom and dad for advice.

"Why don't you do both," they suggested. "There's more time in the day than people realize. Use every minute. You can always catch up on your sleep later."

They were right. As usual.

Acknowledgments

I have benefited greatly from having met and interacted with the people in these tales. To the reader, they may be story characters; to me they are human beings who have brought light and warmth to my life.

My profound appreciation is extended to Peter Golick, simply the wisest man I ever met.

After I helped to teach my daughters, Liz and Lynn, how to swim, the three of us regularly raced together in the pool. One day, when they were teenagers, both girls finished the final lap before I did. They had won for the first time, and I was not to win again. I knew, of course, that swimming was but a metaphor for everything else in life. I was filled with lasting pride and pleasure.

I was fortunate to be inspired by outstanding teachers, among them Harold Akley, Gladys Neal, Ernest Painter, Sam Withers, and the incomparable Kenneth Cameron.

Special thanks go to Gretchen Bennett and to Peter Weis. Peter and Gretchen are two truly creative people who have encouraged, aided and supported my efforts to be one. And thanks for much more besides.

Contemporary writers use the computer; old-fashioned tradition-alists choose the typewriter. Neither for me. A big bold thank you (written with a number two pencil) to Lyn Parker, who utilized modern technology to transform my handwritten scribbles into legible paragraphs.

Introduction

During my teenage years, I came upon a scrapbook. It covered the life of my paternal grandfather, who had died several years before I was born. The scrapbook had been hastily assembled upon the fellow's death. I found it fascinating and believed that it provided me with a sense of my roots and my residual influences. I determined that I would keep a record of my own life, assuming that my future grandchildren might some day receive similar enjoyment and education.

Many decades later, my photographs, newspaper clippings, diplomas, and documents had filled nearly a dozen scrapbooks. They represented the ultimate tribute to my ego and self-gratification. If I had any hopes that my progeny might view me as their humble, introspective, philosophical ancestor, these scrapbooks would never accomplish that objective.

In retirement, I was fortunate to travel extensively with my wife, Joanne. I kept a daily journal, complete not only with observations on our adventures and places visited, but also with my insights, astute and otherwise. Later, upon re-reading the hundreds of pages of the transcribed accounts, I discovered that the reactions they engendered in me were primarily boredom and a propensity to yawn. I could just imagine what the attitude toward them might be from those who had far less involvement with the trips than I did. I shelved my plan to gift the journals to my descendants.

So, reader, may you enjoy these stories. If so, I am very pleased. If not, at least revel in your escape from pounds of thick scrapbooks and pages of interminable travel experiences.

The Stories

While the stories are based on actual events, some names have been changed to protect individuals' privacy.

The ending of "The Love Rock" is imaginary.

Prior to the printing of this book, several of the stories were submitted to magazines. As of the date of printing, the following have been published:

"The Star Spangled Serengeti," in the Fall, 2002 issue of Vermont Ink.

"The Star Spangled Serengeti," in the Fall/Winter 2002-03 issue of Potomac Review, adapted under the title of "An Elder on the Plain."

"The Star Spangled Serengeti," in the Winter, 2002 issue of Aim, America's Intercultural Magazine, with photographs, under the title of "The Serengeti Perspective."

"The Love Rock," in the May, 2003 issue of The Villager.

"Invitation to Hollywood," in the Summer, 2003 issue of Heroes from Hackland, under the title of "James Cagney, Mae Clarke...and Me."

"Separate Rooms," in the September, 2003 issue of True Love.

Role Model

I arose from my folding chair on the auditorium stage and stepped to the podium. Fred Thompson had flattered me with an extravagant introduction.

A few days before, he had told me what he expected. "Inspire them for about twenty minutes," Fred had said. "Just don't make your speech too long. Remember that kids start to fidget after fifteen minutes or so."

Fred was the President of the local Boy Scout Council. He had recruited me to be the keynote speaker at this ceremony at which the oldest of the county's Cub Scouts would graduate to Boy Scout status.

I had achieved Eagle Scout rank in my own scouting days a half-century before, and I had been a staff member for several seasons at Boy Scout camp. However, my real qualification for being selected to speak was the relationship I had with Brendan and his buddies.

Upon retirement, I had joined the Big Brothers organization. In addition to serving as a member of their local Board of Directors, I was assigned a Little Brother. Brendan had lost his father the previous year, and his mother, Sarah, thought he might benefit from a male role model. He and I went canoeing on the river; I took him and his friends bowling; and we spent rainy Saturdays together at the movies. Along the way, Sarah had called on me to help out with some of the scout activities, and I had met Fred Thompson. Brendan and

Sarah would be in the audience tonight as he made the transition from Cub to Boy Scout.

Upon reaching the podium, I retrieved from my jacket pocket the index cards on which I had scribbled the notes I would use for my speech. I glanced at the audience, the forty or so scouts, accompanied by their parents and siblings.

I winked at Sarah and Brendan and began talking. As requested, I had prepared a speech intended to inspire the boys. Dare, share, and care, I would tell them. Dare to do things differently; share your good luck with the less fortunate; care about others. I thought the rhyming mnemonic worked pretty well, and with only five minutes devoted to each point, I could finish before the audience lost attention.

I glanced down at the index card, looked out at the audience, and talked about daring. My words were ones I had prepared, but, as I fixed my eyes on one chubby-cheeked eleven year old boy, I thought back about myself at that age.

We crouched in the high grasses of the dry, overgrown fields that covered so much of Scarsdale. An older boy gave the signal, and those of us with matches struck them carefully against the matchbox strip. Soon the fields were ablaze, and we were ready to run.

"Let's go," another kid yelled. There were about a dozen of us, fourth, fifth, and sixth graders. This was the third time we had engaged in this activity since the school year began, and we knew exactly how far we needed to run and how soon the fire trucks would arrive. Less than thirty minutes later, the firemen were frenetically

Role Model

hosing down the flames, and our group was milling around, offering to assist.

"Haven't I seen you here before?" one of the firemen said to me.

"Sure. We're always here to help," I replied, buoyed with confidence from the presence of my comrades. The thrill of setting the fires was complemented by the power to produce a parade of fire trucks, arriving with sirens blasting. The final satisfaction was feigning innocence as the firemen investigated the fire.

However, the following day in school, the principal had lined up all the boys in the three grades and was sternly addressing us.

"I know you boys are responsible for the scourge of fires," he snarled. "Unless the ringleaders step forward right now, you will all be punished." Mr. Hare was tall, but at this moment he looked enormous.

I giggled nervously.

"I thought so. You come forward," he snapped at me.

I felt dizzy. I didn't know whether to admit my role or not, but my indecision saved me. Mrs. Andrews, my fifth grade teacher, turned to the principal. "He always giggles when he's nervous. He's a good boy. I'm sure he's not responsible for the problem," she asserted softly. I would be indebted to her for the rest of my life.

"Well, if this happens again, we'll keep all of you after school every day until Thanksgiving," Mr. Hare responded. Our fire-setting days were finished; they had been exciting, daring escapades.

My thoughts returned to the auditorium. I was finishing my comments on daring to do things differently. Brendan was beaming up at me, so I was doing all right. I flipped the index card over. "Share your good fortune," the card instructed. I remembered well what "sharing" meant to me when I was a boy.

It was a month after our field fires had ended. The warm September days had evolved to cool fall weather. Halloween was now upon us. My friends and I were this year too "grown up" to go trick or treating. My younger brother would still be costumed, ringing doorbells house to house, collecting candy. I wore my big kid status proudly as I met with my buddies, most of whom were a year or two older. We developed our plans for the evening and solemnly pledged not to turn on one another if we were caught by the police. It was the ultimate sharing.

First, we soaped the windows of an abandoned house, and then those of the nearby farm stand. Next, we made our way to the top of the longest road in the neighborhood. We were looking for houses with windows to soap, but the serendipitous sighting of a car parked on the street presented us with another idea. Magically, the automobile was unlocked, and one of our group crawled into its front seat, then released the parking brake, and shifted the gear into neutral. He exited the car.

"Push," someone yelled.

We pushed the car from the rear and watched the vehicle head down the slight incline. It came to rest opposite a house down the street.

This was great fun. We found two more cars that were unlocked and could be pushed as we made our way down the road. However, the last car crashed into a telephone pole, and, as we were nervously surveying the damage, flashing lights indicated that a police cruiser was upon us.

"Run," was the cry from our group. I was already moving fast. My friend, Jeff, and I headed in the same direction toward our homes a mile away.

"You two, stop," a policeman shouted. All I could think about was the fury I would face from my parents if I were caught. I was not about to halt under any circumstance.

Jeff and I reached the woods behind the houses on our street with the policeman still in pursuit. As we entered the woods, there was a loud crack, the unmistakable sound of a gunshot. Was the policeman firing at us or just into the air? I didn't know. I suddenly thought I was too young to die. Would my parents miss me? Would my friends cry at my funeral? Would my brother be excited about getting my baseball cards and comic books? I kept running. It seemed to take forever before I completed my trip through the woods and arrived home. For years afterward, Jeff and I shared the memory as our most frightening experience.

I returned to the present and looked out at the hundred people in the auditorium. My eyes fixed on Sarah. She was smiling and holding Brendan's hand. My prepared words about sharing seemed to have resonated with the audience.

My next index card read, "Care about others." As I began speaking my rehearsed words, I thought about a time many years before.

I had just finished sixth grade, and the Quaker Ridge neighborhood had outgrown our little school. In September, we would shift to a newly-constructed, normal-sized school. For now, however, all we had known was our four-room schoolhouse, three rooms on the ground level and an additional one in the basement next to the boiler room. Each of the four classrooms housed two grades, and the playground was just large enough for a cramped game of kickball at recess.

My class had completed six years in the old two-grades-to-a-room schoolhouse the day before. My girlfriend, Carolyn, my friend, Stanley, his girlfriend, Marilyn, and I were hanging out at out favorite spot in the fields on this Saturday afternoon in June. School was out; the four-room schoolhouse that had been our daytime home for the past six years was suddenly ours no more; and we were experiencing first love. Using the empty beer bottle we had brought along for the purpose, we formed a four-person circle and played "spin-the-bottle."

After about an hour, the four of us were feeling an increased sense of intimacy from our illicit behavior. We pledged unending love for one another.

"Those were great years," I said of our time at the old schoolhouse.

Role Model

"I loved that place," Carolyn said.

"I hated it," Marilyn responded. We all laughed.

"Let's go back there," Stan suggested.

So, emboldened by our closeness, we hurried through the fields to the school, opened the unlocked door, and sneaked inside. It was eerie to be in the familiar setting with no one else around. We approached blackboards on which we had struggled with arithmetic problems and from which we had learned to spell and to use proper grammar. Now, we scrawled swear words with the well-used chalk. We followed this with overturning desks in each of the classrooms.

Not yet satisfied, we needed to do more for the old schoolhouse's valediction. Using the window poles that were in each room, we struck the lights that were suspended in orderly fashion from the ceiling. The large glass lights swung from side to side, then smashed, and fell like piñatas in pieces to the floor. By the time we left the building, the destruction was complete. The four of us had connected with one another and had bid farewell, in our own fashion, to the school.

A few days later, the local newspaper published their lead story about the appalling vandalism at the school. It became a major subject of conversation in the village, and my parents, among others, opined that it had to be the work of outsiders, because no one in Scarsdale would do such a thing. They would never learn otherwise.

I had finished my prepared words on caring for one another, and I brought my speech promptly to a close staying within the allotted time. I looked out at the audience that was enthusiastically applauding. Somehow, my thoughts that had drifted back to childhood arson, carwrecking, and vandalism apparently had not interfered with the communication.

After Fred Thompson wrapped up the evening's program, I made my way to Brendan and Sarah. They thanked me for my speech and I congratulated Brendan on his becoming a Boy Scout.

As I neared the door to leave, Fred caught up with me. "Wonderful job," he said graciously. "I didn't see any fidgeting. The boys received so much benefit from those inspiring words."

I expressed my thanks.

He continued. "Somehow, though, kids today just aren't as upstanding as we were, not as respectful of authority. I hope this generation will find their way."

"Oh, I think they'll measure up okay," I said as I waved good night.

The Arsonist

Poetry and Ping Pong

After my classes were finished each day, I would walk across the campus to the building housing the college post office and collect my mail. It was not an unpleasant regimen. It allowed me to leave academics and connect with the real world. I always anticipated turning the two combination knobs on my mailbox, opening the little door, and discovering what might be there for me.

In truth, I was usually disappointed. The box's contents were typically, some form of reminder, which intentionally or not had the effect of generating guilty feelings in me. Frequently, the box was cluttered with the spam of that era, notifications of meetings of college clubs which I hadn't joined or information about visiting lecturers or special events that I should attend but wouldn't. Any personal correspondence was generally from my parents or from girls (as they preferred to be called back then; today they would be "women") whom I was dating or from Professor Allen.

The letters from my parents were newsy accounts of their social life or their travels. The breezy tone was inevitably spoiled by the last paragraph, which ended with their admonition: "We hope your marks are improving. Remember why you went to college." Even from a distance, parental love reminded me of my lack of sterling academic achievement.

The mail from girlfriends was instantly identifiable. The blue or pink or beige envelopes were addressed in carefully rounded penmanship; they would be magically scented if the sender were avid enough. After a couple of paragraphs informing me in excruciating detail about life in Northampton or South Hadley, the Smith or Mt. Holyoke correspondent would make mention of the wonderful time she and I had together last month. The nudge was intended to be subtle, but the message was clear. "Why haven't I heard from you?"

The reminders from Professor Allen were more direct. Each student had been assigned a faculty advisor from the department in which he majored, and Professor Allen, who chaired the English Department, had advisory responsibility for me. His letters arrived every three weeks or so and usually requested that I meet with him to discuss my "progress." These resulted in uncomfortable meetings in which I stuttered through lame explanations of why I had not lived up to his high expectations of me.

I attended college in the 1950's at Trinity in Hartford. My major collegiate accomplishment was becoming the best ping-pong player on campus, and I balanced a minimal level of scholarship with all manner of nonacademic behavior. Now, I was in my junior year, more than half way through a rather unexceptional undergraduate experience.

It was a frigid January day in New England. I had walked from the other side of campus across the Quad, down the Long Walk to the post office. The blast of hot air was welcoming as I entered the building and hurried down the stairs. I had suffered through four long classes beginning early in the morning, and I was looking forward to returning to my room after checking my mail.

I turned the combination knobs and opened the mailbox. There were none of the usual letters nor any event notifications. There was only one lone envelope, the long white kind I associated with business communications. I looked at it closely. My full name was typed in formal fashion, and the return address in the upper left corner read, "The Imperial Palace, Tokyo." This had to be a mistake or perhaps a joke. It was just twelve years after the horrific atomic bombings on Hiroshima and Nagasaki, only sixteen years since the attack on Pearl Harbor. College students didn't receive letters from Tokyo. I didn't know anyone in Japan and most certainly knew no one at the Imperial Palace. I opened the envelope.

The enclosed letter was indeed intended for me. It was dated in late December and noted that the committee for the Upcoming New Year's Poetry Party took pleasure in informing me that my poem "has been duly laid before their Majesties The Emperor and Empress." It went on to describe the Poetry Party and Emperor Hirohito's love of "Waka" poetry.

Suddenly, I remembered. A couple of months earlier, with an exam scheduled for the following day, I had been spending an evening in escape from the necessary studying. My roommate, Carl, had left for the library after dinner, as was his habit. I had found no other wayward comrades for ping-pong competition, and I was browsing through magazines for diversion. Scanning the current issue of Time magazine, I had come across a blurb in their Miscellany section, describing to readers the Emperor's New Year's Poetry Party and humorously inviting poetic submissions. Finding this event half a world away infinitely more interesting than my upcoming Macro Economics exam, I had dashed off my version of a poem and had mailed it to Tokyo. By the next day, the realities of academic life had once again surfaced, and I had forgotten all about the poem. As I stood before my mailbox, I thought about the contrast between my undergraduate life and a Poetry Party hosted by the Emperor of Japan on the other side of the earth.

Upon arriving back at my room, I encountered my roommate working at his desk. One of Carl's activities was as a weekly columnist for the college newspaper, the Tripod. In the eternal fashion of newspaper columnists, he had a deadline the next morning and a blank page in front of him. There are just too many weeks in a school year for easy subjects for a lifestyle columnist to focus upon. I showed him my letter from Japan, and we shared a laugh over the absurdity of my having received it.

An hour passed and Carl had made no progress on his column. Displaying his desperation, he asked me to show him the letter once again. "You realize this is just a form letter," I said, indicating the obvious about the politely worded communication that had my name typed in appropriate places between the printed portions of the letter. Carl was silent, as he began to write his column.

When the Tripod was published later that week, Carl's column was featured prominently. It began, "Trinity College's literary community is buzzing over the notification from Japan received by one of its own". It indicated that my poem had been "chosen in an internationally recognized contest to be recited before the Emperor and Empress at a momentous gathering of the Imperial Court on New Year's Day." Carl had gone on to amplify the story, with "many aspiring Japanese and foreign writers are presented for consideration and Their Majesties select the best literary effort." In case any reader were not to appreciate its importance, the column closed with the assertion that the New Year's Day event was to be "the high point in the Japanese literary-social calendar."

The Poetry Party had been transformed into a poetry contest. While the column didn't explicitly state I had been the winner of the contest, that was the clear implication. Carl had written his Trinity Tripod column with his tongue firmly in his cheek. Where satire ended and fantasy began wasn't altogether clear, but the column began a series of events that neither of us could have ever imagined.

The Hartford Courant is the Connecticut capital's morning newspaper. It was founded by Benjamin Franklin in 1764 and is the nation's oldest continuously published newspaper. The Courant subscribes to the Tripod, so that in the event of any important event at Trinity, it could run the story. This way, it complements its national and state coverage with significant local news.

A few days later, I received a telephone call from a reporter from the Courant. "I would appreciate talking with you. Where on campus could I meet with you," he asked.

The Hartford Courant wanted to interview me. I had no idea what I could say to a reporter who thought this was a news story. "Let's meet at the Trinity library," I suggested, as if I knew the place well.

So, following my meeting with the reporter, the Courant ran a lengthy and enthusiastic article February 3rd. It described the New Year's event not as a party but as a contest, fully accepting the

Tripod's version. It discussed "waka" poetry in detail, using the information gleaned from the letter to me. I had told the reporter that I had written the poem in only fifteen minutes, and he had emphasized that fact with the headline "Poem Trinity Man Wrote in a Hurry in Royal Contest in Japan."

Two days after the Hartford Courant article appeared, I was interviewed by a reporter from the Hartford Times, the city's afternoon newspaper. Looking for a fresh angle to the story, the Times reporter found it when he asked to see a copy of the poem, and I told him quite truthfully that I hadn't kept a copy. He was incredulous. "I never keep copies of my poetry," I shrugged. I was now not only a poet but I was developing a reputation for quirkiness as well. The Times article appeared a few days later, focusing on my diffidence toward international acclaim.

The following week I received a call from WTIC, Channel 3, the CBS television channel in Hartford. They wanted to tape me for their news show that evening. They requested that I come to their studio later that afternoon for the taping. They told me the questions they would be asking so that I might be prepared.

It was time now for me to really use the library. During the next four hours, I learned about Japanese poetry. "Waka" poems have 31 syllables, arranged 5-7-5-7-7. "Waka" is an ancient form much loved by traditionalists such as Emperor Hirohito. Only later was the more familiar haiku developed with its seventeen syllable form. Most of these poems, extraordinarily short by Western standards, deal with nature or are elegies or reveries. Typically they don't stand up well to translation out of Japanese, the ultimate irony in my circumstance.

I also learned about Emperor Hirohito. To most Americans at that time, he represented Japan and its bellicosity in World War II. However, to the Japanese people, his status was truly godlike. He and his ancestors had ruled Japan seemingly forever, and he had been 124th in direct lineage to the throne. His reign had begun in 1926. Under U.S. occupation in 1946, Hirohito renounced his legendary divinity and most of his powers to become a democratic constitutional monarch. He was to continue in that position until his death in 1989.

My television interview went well, especially because I was not asked either to speak Japanese or how I could have written a Japanese poem. I was queried on the subject matter of my poem, and I answered "the aesthetic quality of light," the same response I had used in each of the newspaper interviews. This was essentially the truth as the long-forgotten Time magazine piece had indicated that this year's subject would be on "the quality of light." My enhanced response was intended to forestall further questioning on this aspect of the subject, and as usual, it worked. Most of the questions that the interviewer asked were about me and how I was handling my celebrity status. I answered with the humility that was indeed appropriate.

Viewers of the February 14th Channel 3 Nightly News watched the taped interview that evening. I learned later that a two-minute excerpt was used as well on the CBS National News. At about the same time, the Associated Press picked up the story from The

Hartford Courant and articles describing my contest success began appearing in newspapers throughout the country.

For weeks afterward, my parents were to hear from friends from coast to coast who saw me on CBS or who read about me, courtesy of the Associated Press. When my mother received an excited telephone call about it from her sister three thousand miles away, I moved up several notches in parental estimation. I was to be freed from any more letters from home with advice to "remember why you went to college."

The publicity had spread from college to the Hartford community to national acclaim and now back to increased campus celebrity. My professors, who previously had scant reason to take notice of me, now treated me with deference. Even Professor Allen asked me to stand up in Linguistics class to applause as he noted my proficiency in literary Japanese. I never knew how he could relate that to a student he had previously associated with dangling participles and split infinitives in our native language.

My college academic career took a turn for the better. Perhaps my professors saw me differently and my responses to essay questions on exams were judged to have a certain sophistication that hadn't been observed previously. Or, maybe, I responded to the need to live up to a new status on campus. Nevertheless, I continued to be true to myself. I avoided the library unless absolutely necessary and I concentrated on perfecting my spin serve at the ping-pong table.

The Japanese poetry contest defined my college years to my mother. Despite my protestations, she would assert to all who would listen, "My son's a poet. At college he won an international poetry contest."

In middle age, I took my first trip to Japan as a tourist. I struggled to learn a few Japanese words that I could use in Tokyo. As I repeated "arigatou" and "matane" and "oisie," finally committing them to memory, I remembered with a smile having received Professor Allen's congratulations in class for my fluency in literary Japanese.

Carl's journalism career ended with his Tripod column. He went on to become a prominent lawyer in the Hartford area. He and I and our wives get together now from time to time to socialize, reminisce and debate current events. The last time we were together, Carl and I argued about some political matter. I made a point and backed it up with information from a news article in the New York Times. I thought I had made my case.

Carl paused a moment, then had the last word. "Don't believe everything you read in the newspapers," he declared.

KUNAICHO
IMPERIAL PALACE
TOKYO

Mr. Everett E. Elting, Jr.

The Committee for the New Year's Poetry Party
at the Imperial Court of Japan,
Imperial Palace,
Tokyo

The Committee for the New Year's Poetry Party at the Imperial Court takes pleasure
in informing   Mr. Everett E. Elting, Jr,

that   his   poem which was sent in for the New Year's Poetry Party, 1957,
has been duly laid before T. M. The Emperor and Empress.

For information, the Poetry Party annually held at the Imperial Court at the New
Year is a ceremony at which are officially presented the poems composed on a theme
previously given in a traditional Japanese poetry form of 'Waka' (a special poetry form
consisting of 31 syllables in Japanese, or of five word-groups with 5, 7, 5, 7, 7, syllables
respectively). Not only the poems of H. M. The Emperor and other members of the
Imperial family but also those selected from among the poems sent in for the contest
will be recited before Their Majesties at the Party. All the poems for the Party have to
be in the form of 'Waka.'

The poems written by foreigners in their own languages as in this case would be
filed and only presented to H. M. The Emperor after the Poetry Party is over.

January   11th, 1957.

Fame has an innocuous beginning

Poet with Mom, Brother Pete, and Dad

The Love Rock

I pressed down a little harder on the gas as I turned east from Manchester and headed the car toward Stratton Mountain. This stretch was the Vermont version of a highway, three well-paved lanes, with rest areas for photo takers. After several minutes of uphill climb, it turned into a winding, narrow access road, which covers the final distance to the mountain. The drive is a familiar one for the skiers who travel up from New York on winter weekends as well as for the tourists who make Stratton their destination during the summer and at foliage time. Nearly all of them are awed by the beauty of the scenery, particularly during those last few miles.

I had made that trip countless times through the years. I always felt a special exhilaration as I drove the final leg. The towering mountains on either side contrasted with the slim ribbon of road, making the journey especially exciting as I drove along the familiar curving route.

But there was one particular point along the way that was extra-ordinary. Upon rounding a bend, jutting out from the right about a hundred feet ahead was an enormous rock that was unusually shaped. Time and the harsh Vermont climate had eroded it in a fashion that gave the gray mass the square-jawed, high-browed features of an Indian chief.

Very little imagination was required to notice the resemblance between the craggy rock and a tough, old chieftain. I always delighted in coming around the curve and experiencing the striking sight of the Indian head. And it awakened in me a creative dream. Some day I would paint that rock; the curious shape would become a brightly-colored Indian face. I would dedicate the creation to my beloved as a sign of my affection for all the passers-by to see.

Well, that kind of dream would have to be fulfilled sometime in the future. For now, I had no beloved. I had recently broken up with my girlfriend, and I was in Vermont by myself for the weekend. I had driven the four-hour trip from Manhattan early Saturday morning, and I had arrived just in time for a doubles tennis game in the cool September air. My friends and I arranged to meet at the Stratton Tennis Center at noon, and I had traveled in my tennis clothes so as to be on time. Labor Day weekend traffic inevitably lengthens the trip, and I arrived with only a few minutes to spare.

Nevertheless, I made it. The three guys I was playing with had come up to Stratton after work the day before and were awaiting my arrival. The tennis match had become an annual tradition for us, and we always scheduled three hours of court time.

We alternated partners, eventually playing two sets with each of the other guys, six sets in all. The tennis was of a pretty high caliber, and we attracted a bit of a crowd. My first serve was going in, and my net play was crisp.

By about the fourth set, I noticed her. She wore tennis clothes, and she was standing with some other people. She was very attractive, and, while she wasn't watching as intently as I would have liked, she did seem to be observing me. My game picked up, and I finished with a win.

As the match ended and we left the court, I was feeling good. I walked past her boldly, hoping for a compliment on my play.

"Well, you're sure no Jimmy Connors," she said, looking me straight in the eye.

"How about some lunch," was all I could think to reply.

She laughed. "If you want to invite me to lunch, you should do it before the middle of the afternoon."

"Dinner is what I meant. What's your name?"

"I'm Chris," she teased. "And I'll call you Jimmy if you keep working on your backhand." She smiled with her eyes.

Jimmy Connors had won the U.S. Open the year before. He had made the two-handed backhand respectable, and I had recently begun using it. Chris Evert was the best female tennis player in the world at the time, and it was public knowledge that the two were romantically involved.

So, on Saturday night of Labor Day weekend, I had dinner with her. She had dark hair and dark eyes that were never still. I felt more alive than I had in ages.

By the end of dinner, I learned that this was her first time in Vermont, and she was here with friends. I was pleased to hear that she had no man in her life. We were still calling each other Chris and Jimmy, concealing our real identities. It had the effect of raising the level of romance and mystery.

After dinner, we went to the Equinox Hotel, and we listened to music and drank stingers on the rocks. She said that she had never seen a town as lovely as Manchester, and I told her of its history.

Long before the area became a major destination for skiers, Manchester was a chic nineteenth century summer resort. I recounted how Ethan Allen had conspired with his Green Mountain Boys for Vermont statehood in the Equinox Hotel Tavern. I explained to her that Abraham Lincoln had booked into the Equinox for a month during the summer of 1865, a vacation that had been cancelled by John Wilkes Booth's bullet.

We talked, and we talked. Later, with encouragement from the stingers, I suggested we forego the accommodations with our respective friends and take a room together at the Equinox. She responded that she didn't want to be responsible for my assassination.

"It's too soon," she told me with real feeling. I knew she was right, but I was looking forward to the future with great anticipation.

It was late when I drove her back to Stratton to the rooms she was sharing with her friends. We arranged to meet the following morning. I was enchanted by her. She had a liveliness and a caring way that I had seldom encountered. I knew something important was happening to me. We had spent an evening getting to know each other, and I was completely taken by her. I could tell she liked me too.

We played tennis on Sunday morning. She played an excellent game and I told her so. "I guess you'll just have to keep calling me Chrissie," she said.

After lunch we went canoeing on the Batten Kill, one of the country's famous trout streams. With birds darting from the trees on the river's banks, we successfully navigated the small rapids. When I pointed out that lesser boatmen than I might have capsized, she promptly shifted her weight and overturned the canoe. We were drenched and loved it.

After a change of clothes, we went to dinner at the Toll Gate Lodge, one of my favorite restaurants anywhere. We sat next to a large window and watched the mountain brook trickle through its streambed. For the first time, we talked seriously. She told me that she was close to her parents, and her father was quite ill. Because of his illness, this weekend was her first happy time in ages, she said, and meeting me was the best thing that had happened to her in a long time.

For my part, I told her about the importance of the Indian head rock. I had shown it to her earlier in the day, but now I described my dream to her. When I fell in love, I would paint the rock to capture my lover's features. It would be the head of an Indian chief, but the eyes would match those of my lover. She listened silently.

As dinner came to an end, we were holding hands. I was entranced. She was fun; she was exciting; she was warm and tender. I was sure she was passionate as well. I knew we would make love that night.

Suddenly, her friends came rushing into the restaurant. They had been searching for her for the past hour. Her father had taken a turn for the worse, and they must take her back to the city immediately. They had packed her things in their car, and it was ready to go.

The three of them hurried out of the restaurant toward their car. I said that I would pay the bill and meet them outside. It took much longer that I had expected, and by the time I reached the parking area, they had left.

She was gone from my life. I often wondered at what point she realized that neither one of us knew how to get in touch with the other. And many times, I thought about what might have been.

Later that year, two other events took place. I turned 30, and I was transferred by my company to Los Angeles.

L.A. is a long way from Vermont – spiritually as well as geographically. During the years that followed, New York and Vermont were replaced in my mind by my career and by my new wife, a fine woman who prefers travel to tennis and cooking to canoeing.

I think my life is quite happy, but, just recently, I persuaded Allison to take a week's trip to Vermont, so that I might revisit a former time. We drove through Manchester, where designer outlets had replaced country stores, and asphalt pavement had been laid on dirt roads. The Equinox Hotel sported fresh paint and new shutters and the Toll Gate Lodge had been renamed Mistral's Restaurant. The changes were dramatic, but the quaint Vermont village continued to evoke my memories of long ago.

As I was showing Allison some of my old haunts, we drove from Manchester to Stratton. We approached that long forgotten bend in the road, and I suddenly remembered the old rock. I began to tell my wife about the strange rock that looks like an Indian chief.

And then I saw it. To my amazement, it was painted. Much of the color had faded, but clearly it had been painted. "Why it kind of looks like you," Allison exclaimed. "It has your eyes and your features. Isn't that something!"

I abruptly pulled over to the side of the road and stopped the car. While my wife asked me "what on earth are you doing," I got out of the car to look at the rock more closely. Time had weathered the paint, but it must have been beautiful some years before. Then, I noticed a not-quite-legible telephone number high over one ear.

Allison honked the horn, and I turned and walked to the car.

I drove a little slower the rest of the way to Stratton.

The Indian Head Rock

Cold War Warriors

Carefully, I parked my Nash Rambler in the Cedar Knolls parking lot. The car was brand new, my first automobile. I had purchased it earlier that week before driving to the Air Force base. I registered at the front desk at the Knolls, the only weekly stay facility in the city of Holyoke. I had arrived that day at Westover Air Force Base in Massachusetts where I had been assigned after completing Personnel Officers School at Lackland in San Antonio. The light snow that was falling and the cold March air represented a dramatic change from the southern Texas climate from which I had come.

The times were different from today. "Terrorism" was not part of the vernacular; the world crises were all offshore. We were competing with the Russians on every level, arms buildup, space exploration, and international alliances, but there had been no major fighting for five years. The hopes were for peace for some time to come.

It was the spring of 1959. I had graduated from college the preceding June. Coincident with graduation, I had been commissioned as a lieutenant in the Air Force, with orders to report to Lackland Air Force Base, Texas in October, 1958, by direction of the President. The President was Dwight Eisenhower, and in the post-Korean War period, military service was considered to be a patriotic duty. Either young men submitted to the draft or, as thousands of us elected to do, became officers through college ROTC programs.

Our official documents indicated that our "commissions would continue in force at the pleasure of the President of the United

States of America." Practically speaking, that meant that, after graduation, we would be giving the country three years of our lives as officers, a fair trade-off, rather than being drafted soldiers for twenty-four months.

Upon graduation from Personnel School, we had been permitted to choose our destinations based upon our class standing. Spending my evenings studying personnel regulations instead of drinking at the Officers' Club had paid off for me, since my class rank enabled me to select Westover, only ten miles from Judy, who was in her junior year at Smith College in Northampton.

I had parked my car next to a bright red Ford Thunderbird convertible in the parking lot and unpacked my duffel bag. My accommodation was a bedroom and sitting room with a galley kitchen. It was modest, but it was far better than had I been housed in the bachelor officers' quarters on the base.

"Hi, may I come in," a voice inquired. I had left my suite door slightly ajar.

"Sure," I responded. I opened the door. The visitor was tall and slim and well tanned. His smile was friendly.

"It seems that both of us checked in today, so I thought we should get to know each other," he said.

Ken was a couple years older than I was. He had been in the Air Force for three years and was a pilot, having completed flight school before arriving at Westover. He told me he was considering making the Air Force his career, an option I would never have considered for myself. Ken's father and uncle owned the two largest Ford dealerships on Long Island, and as Ken put it succinctly, "If you knew my father and my uncle, you'd rather spend your career flying jets than driving Fords off the lot."

I told him a little about myself and how I had chosen Westover. "Judy and I will probably become engaged this summer, and we'll get married when she graduates next year," I shared with him.

"She must be pretty special," Ken said.

We congratulated one another on having manipulated off-base accommodations. While the Cedar Knolls wasn't exactly paradise, it provided us with a freedom we never could have achieved if we were confined to the base. The red convertible, it turned out, was his, and, with each of us having cars, transportation was not a problem. The Air Force paid a housing allowance to officers living off base. It had been a good day for both of us.

Westover was the headquarters of the Eighth Air Force's 57th Air Division, a key unit of the Strategic Air Command. SAC was the Air Force's primary offensive capability. Giant B-52 bombers filled the base's hangars, along with KC-135's, tankers designed to refuel the B-52's in mid-air. This allowed the bombers to fly indefinitely, without ever having to land. In total, there were 12,000 Air Force personnel and their families in the base community. During this cold war period, it was an interesting and exciting place to be stationed.

As the junior personnel officer on the base, I was assigned responsibility for the Base Processing Center with forty enlisted men and women reporting to me. Our function was to be the custodians of the base's personnel records and to update them to reflect promotions, assignments, performance reports, and pay grades. My supervisor was a captain, a career officer. All my job required was to insure that the Processing team made few mistakes, didn't lose personnel files, and created no problems for the captain, who was angling for his next promotion.

The morning after my arrival at Westover, I was in my office at the Base Processing Center, organizing my desk. The telephone rang. "Lieutenant," the voice on the other end of the phone began, " we are establishing a course for officers to improve their correspondence skills. You're invited to take the course."

I was a Personnel Officer, and English major in college, and I had my fill of school. The last thing I wanted to do was to take another course. Politely, I said all that to the well-intentioned caller, and we ended the conversation.

Fewer than five minutes had elapsed before the telephone rang again. It was a different caller. He told me that he had been informed that I was eminently qualified to be the instructor in the military correspondence course. " Would you be willing to teach the course," he asked. "We are authorized to offer you a fee over and above your lieutenant's pay."

In five minutes, I had been transformed from student status to instructor with extra pay. It was a heady experience for a fellow who had not yet turned 23.

That night, Ken stopped by my room. "I have an idea," he said. "I saw today that there's a house available for rent. It's a half-mile from the entrance gates to the base. I think it's a nice property, and it would be a good place for you to invite Judy. Unlike this spot." He added. "We could share it, and I think it would suit us well. Let's drive over tomorrow in your nice new car and take a look at it."

Ken's charm was infectious, and his logic made sense. The following day, we looked at the house. It wasn't large, two bedrooms, two bathrooms, a living room, dining room, and kitchen. However, it had a screened porch and a large back yard. By the end of the week, we had moved out of the Cedar Knolls and into the house.

Soon thereafter, spring came to western Massachusetts. I would often drive after work from Chicopee Falls, where Westover was located, to Northampton to visit Judy. She and I would go to dinner at one of the town's restaurants, take in a movie or college activity, and end the evening at a local tavern. On weekends, I would pick her up at Smith, and we would drive back to Ken's and my house, where she would study and relax. On Friday and Saturday nights, we would go often to the Officers' Club for dinner and entertainment.

At the end of the semester, Judy and I became engaged. During the summer, Judy enrolled in Smith's summer school, and we continued to enjoy our easy life, enhanced by the convenience of the house I shared with Ken. There was a marked contrast between Judy's and my life and Ken's lifestyle.

Ken was good-looking, no, actually, extremely good-looking. In addition to the benefit of good genes, his appearance was enhanced by a faithful adherence to thirty minutes each day with a sunlamp and the most unusual diet I ever encountered. Other than a love for Scotch whisky, he allowed himself no caloric intake other than soup. He imbibed scotch regularly and enjoyed a bowl of soup three times a day. He maintained that by alternating soup varieties, his diet provided him with all the nutritional building blocks for good health. I don't know about that, but Ken was always tan and slim. Together with his constant smile, his soft-spoken manner, and his looks, his red convertible provided my pilot housemate with the attributes he needed to attract an untold number of women.

Ken and I hosted barbeques several nights each week that summer with Judy and another woman as our guests. Ken would participate fully in cooking steaks on the grill and then eat only the contents of a can of soup. The woman, Ken's date for the evening, was a different person each time. There were nurses from the base hospital, female Air Force officers, and sometimes the wives of Ken's fellow pilots when their husbands were away on flights to other bases. Our house became infamous at Westover.

Despite Ken's outrageous behavior, I never saw a spurned woman get upset with him nor did I encounter any angry husband of the wives he dated. His charm and juggling skill seemed to always work successfully for him. He and I had an easy friendship despite our dramatically different lifestyles.

My Air Force workdays were going well. The Base Processing Center was doing its job effectively, and my supervisor had just been promoted to major. As 1959 ended, the world was a comparatively peaceful place, and I had no doubt that I had chosen well the means by which I was fulfilling my military obligation.

Judy was now a college senior. My fiancée and my housemate were friendly with one another, if not completely enthusiastic in their relationship. Judy did not approve of Ken's lifestyle, and he, while respectful toward her, didn't understand how I could exchange the opportunities of bachelorhood for the constrictions of impending marriage.

Once, hoping to improve their relationship, I took Ken with me to Smith to see Judy in her environment. Circumstances led to my leaving him at her dormitory while I walked to the college library in search of Judy. I asked two friends of Judy's to look after Ken while I located her. By the time Judy and I returned, an hour had passed. Over the next few weeks, Ken dated both Diane and Sally, the two friends, each without the knowledge of the other or of their boyfriends. My attempt to build an understanding between Judy and Ken had not been entirely successful.

In June of 1960, Judy graduated, and a week later, she and I married. I moved out of the house that Ken and I shared for over a year, and he decided to remain in the house on his own. When I drove past in my Rambler, if I saw the red Thunderbird in the driveway, I would honk a greeting.

Judy and I moved into a home that was a short distance away. The house had been constructed by a local dairy farmer on a corner of his farm. It was a new experience to have cows grazing behind the house, a contrast to the backyard barbeques we had enjoyed down the road. I saw less of Ken now but followed his progress through perusing the personnel records from time to time. His supervisors described him in glowing terms on his performance evaluations, "shows no fear," "excellent with people," and "can accomplish anything he chooses when he sets his mind to it." It was no surprise when Ken achieved an early promotion to captain.

As 1960 came to an end, a new President had been elected. Shortly after John Kennedy's inauguration, Cuban refugees failed ignominiously in their attempt to overthrow Fidel Castro by invading Cuba at the Bay of Pigs. When President Kennedy and the U.S.S.R.'s Chairman Khrushev convened a summit meeting in Vienna in early June of 1961, the Soviet Union presented an ultimatum to the U.S., France, and Britain to exit Berlin. The cold war was definitely heating up.

With tensions increasing, Judy and I departed in July on a long-awaited honeymoon trip to Europe. We drove the Rambler to McGuire Air Force Base in New Jersey and waited for three days until there was space available on an Air Force transport flight. Learning that there were two seats on a flight to Madrid, we scurried on board. From Spain, Judy and I traveled by car and train through France, Germany, Denmark, the Netherlands, and England. Six weeks after we left Westover, we arrived back from our enjoyable, enlightening trip.

We returned to a world that had changed. In mid-August, East Germany had erected the Berlin Wall to prevent the exodus of East Germans from East Berlin to West Berlin. President Kennedy recommended to the American people that families should build and stock underground shelters against the possibility that nuclear weapons would be launched against Americans.

I was only a month away from the completion of my three-year term of duty in the Air Force. It was not to be. On my desk upon our return were new orders for me. "By order of the President, the designated officer's term of duty shall be extended for an indefinite period." I would spend the next year in the Air Force.

In our Base Processing Center procedures, personnel orders were routinely handled by the enlisted people working there. Occasionally, there would be an order that was classified as Secret or Top Secret. I would handle these orders personally since I was the only one at the Processing Center with a Top Secret security clearance. This type of order usually dealt with an individual being Dishonorably Discharged for criminal activity or a high-ranking officer being demoted for inappropriate conduct.

Late one afternoon in September, a Top Secret transfer order came across my desk. I had never seen a transfer requiring this kind of security; something important must be involved.

I opened it and sat there stunned. It was the first order for U.S. pilots to be sent to Viet Nam. Four names were on the list; the first one was Ken's. He was to depart in three days.

Judy would eat dinner without me that night. I would pick up a couple of cans of soup and head over to Ken's to deliver these orders in person. He would not have access to Campbell's where he was going.

While Ken would require more than his legendary charm to survive in the months ahead, he would be all right. For me, personnel files would become more about personnel and less about files. We didn't know it yet, but we would all grow up fast. There would be assassination, demonstrations, and killing, and dying in a distant land. The cold war was coming to its end, and a new era was upon us.

Judy prepares for trip to Europe

May Day Memories

I drove the yellow Dasher station wagon north from Lisbon toward Estoril. The winding road hugged the coastline, and frequently I was headed directly into the sun.

The blazing sunset over the Atlantic was as blinding to my eyes as it was beautiful.

"Look, isn't it gorgeous," my wife, Judy, said to Lynn and Liz who were curled up reading on the back seat. Lynn was ten years old, and Liz, eight. Sunsets, being an adult pleasure, our daughters didn't even look up from their books. Lollipop, the family Scottish terrier, was dozing in the far back of the car. Judy and I would appreciate the view on our own.

"I guess we should be thankful that they don't seem to be bothered by everything that's happening," I offered. It was now early Sunday evening, and indeed our weekend had been filled with harrowing experiences.

As usual, we had made the four-hour trip from our rental home in Estoril to our house in the Algarve on Friday afternoon. Upon arriving, we had been stunned to see the large painted graffiti on the sign outside the entrance to the twenty-dwelling enclave where our house was situated. The sign was obviously intended for us as we were the only foreign homeowners resident in the area. "Vota no PCP; Morte a CIA," it read. The enthusiasm for the Revolution had evolved to increasing aggressiveness, and this message, "Vote for

53

the Portuguese Communist Party; Death to the CIA," was distressingly blunt and personal.

Entering our Algarve driveway, we had found that the letters in our mailbox had been opened and apparently read. There had been no attempt to disguise the invasive action.

"Why on earth would they bother to open my Bloomingdale's catalogue," Judy had asked rhetorically. "As if I would dare to order something from there," she added.

Our telephone in the Algarve house was tapped, as had already been our experience in our villa in Estoril. There were no mechanical listening devices, just the sound of breathing from some anonymous third party.

If all the aggravation were not enough, this afternoon, as we approached the Lisbon Bridge returning from the south, our car was stopped unceremoniously by uniformed men with hammer and sickle armbands. It didn't seem to affect Lynn and Liz, reading in the back as usual. Lollipop responded with mere curiosity. Judy and I, however, were unnerved as the military men asked to see our identification. When we displayed our American passports, the soldiers acted as if they had caught the enemy. Our car was searched thoroughly, presumably for weapons, before they waved us on.

Finally, we reached Estoril, I turned off the coast road, drove up the hill past the casino, and unlocked the big gate at the driveway entrance that guarded our rented villa. Finally, we entered the safety of our weekday home. This last weekend in December, 1974 had begun like most others, but now the political situation was becoming more and more difficult and frightening to us.

Portugal had been governed from the right, a classically fascist county, from 1932 to early 1974. First, António Salazar, then Marcelo Caetano reigned as dictators during this period. On April 25, 1974, the government was overthrown by a military coup; it began in Portugal's African colonies of Mozambique and Angola, and quickly spread to Portugal itself. The coup was dubbed the "flower revolution," because there was no resistance to the soldiers, who wore red carnations instead of carrying guns. The people cheered the end of colonialism and what many hoped might be the beginning of a moderate government and the start of a modern nation.

The Armed Forces Movement, the MFA, was in control, under the leadership of General António Spinola. Independence was granted to the African colonies, censorship was abolished, new elections were promised, and the secret police force was disbanded. General Spinola was inaugurated as President on May 15th.

Despite the promising start, communists, supported by Soviet Russia, sensed an opportunity. With the help of more radical members of the MFA, they usurped power. The country took a sharp turn to the left. General Spinola was removed, banks and insurance companies were nationalized, and land reform was begun, with vast farming estates turned into collectives. The dictatorship on the right was transformed into extremism from the left.

By December of 1974, world attention was focused on this unlikely nation. American concern had reached genuine fear. Portugal was a NATO country, and the U. S. was worried about NATO bases and secrets falling into Soviet hands. Moreover, no western European country had ever gone communist; that precedent was one that the United States could not allow to happen. American businessmen left Portugal and went home. They were replaced by CIA agents who entered the country in significant numbers.

Our family's interest in Portugal had begun several years before. After developing great affection toward the lovely, peaceful country and its gentle people, we had built a small casa. The home was situated high on the Algarve cliffs, with ocean views in three directions, a large pool, and fruit trees in the garden. Outside the picturesque town of Lagos, it was the perfect vacation villa for us, and we rented it to American tourists during the months that we were not using it.

The whole family had enjoyed our time in the Algarve. Judy cherished the warm summers when she and the girls could escape to the vacation home. She delighted in buying fish for dinner directly from the fishermen as they docked with their morning catch; she scurried daily to the bakery to pick up the bread, still hot from the oven; and she practiced her Portuguese while bargaining for vegetables at the farm market.

Liz and Lynn loved making their daily choice of either taking the walk down to one of several beaches or staying at the house with its free-form swimming pool. Either way, there were kids of many nationalities in the surrounding houses, and they played and learned from one another.

Judy taught school in the New York suburb of Chappaqua where we lived, and the girls attended the same school. Her vacations coincided with theirs, and the three of them spent significant time at the Algarve house in the summers. I joined them for two or three weeks and dreamed of finding an entrepreneurial opportunity that would allow me to combine worthwhile income with our fulltime enjoyment of the idyllic Portuguese lifestyle.

In late 1973, I had received a telephone call from a friend who knew of my interest in Portugal. He oversaw worldwide franchising for Kentucky Fried Chicken. KFC owned or franchised their operations in every western European country except Portugal, and each was a growing, successful enterprise. Now, they were preparing to award the Portuguese franchise. The ideal franchisee would be a combination of a well-positioned Portuguese company to finance the expansion and a successful American marketing person who knew Portugal to run the operation. Was I interested?

Of course, I was.

By early 1974, I had met twice with my new Portuguese partners, once in New York and once in Lisbon. We quickly reached an agreement; my partners would finance the operation, I would manage it, and we would share the profits.

Judy and I placed our Chappaqua home on the market and sold it with its furniture. On May 1st, Judy told the school district that she wanted a year's sabbatical from her teaching job and likely would not be returning after that time. On the same day, I resigned my position as Vice President of Marketing at the conglomerate where I was employed. Soon, thereafter, I flew to Kentucky for several weeks of orientation to KFC.

Judy and I attended one farewell party after another. We were fulfilling the fantasies of friends and colleagues to live in an exotic land and to have an extremely lucrative business opportunity. Our small villa would no doubt be overscheduled with American visitors. As the four of us and Lollipop flew to newly liberated Portugal, with General Spinola as President, we felt excited, adventuresome, and fortunate.

Upon arriving in Lisbon, we acquired the new Volkswagen Dasher that we had arranged to be shipped from Germany. It would become Judy's car. She and the girls moved into our villa in the Algarve. I rented a small apartment in Estoril, where I stayed during the week.

I started work immediately. I completed the Kentucky Fried Chicken market research projects I had begun prior to our arrival in the country and scouted locations for possible restaurants. Each Friday afternoon I made the four-hour drive to the Algarve in my company car, and I would return early Monday morning in time to start the workday at my office in Lisbon.

Our weekends were everything we had anticipated. There was caldo verde, the great Portuguese soup, and grilled sardines upon my arrival on Friday night, and we would bring one another up-to-date on our week's activities. After dinner, there was time for a swim or a walk along the Atlantic cliffs to the beautiful rock formations of Ponta da Piedade, with Lollipop leading the way. On Saturday and Sunday, we enjoyed the beach or played tennis and visited the local gypsy market or a traveling circus or fair. Saturday night, we went to one or another of the extraordinary restaurants in Lagos or nearby Portimao; the four of us would dine in memorable fashion for under $20.00.

Our Portuguese dream had become a reality, but it was short-lived. By October, General Spinola had been overthrown, and the communists were in power, aided by the "young captains," junior officers of the MFA whose far left leanings resulted from years of repressive dictatorship. Our tapped telephones and intercepted mail formed an unsettling backdrop in a country where easygoing, friendly people as much as the beautiful scenery had framed our world.

Liz and Lynn continued to enjoy their life, but Judy and I would begin all our telephone conversations between Estoril and the Algarve with "How are you? Is everything okay?" The political climate was deteriorating, and, increasingly, we were becoming concerned.

So, in early December, Judy and the girls moved up to Estoril. The town, thirty minutes' drive from Lisbon, was a beach resort unlike any other. The large houses, hidden behind high stone walls, were home to innumerable deposed royalty, exiled kings, marquesses from Italy, princesses from Romania and Russia, and baronesses from Germany. The count of Barcelona, the queen of Bulgaria, and the sister of the pretender to the Portuguese throne all lived there. On any given night, several of them could be seen at Europe's largest casino, the centerpiece of Estoril. The staid, somewhat stuffy atmosphere of the fabled casino would soon be disturbed by Lollipop's daily unleashed sojourns through the casino's gardens.

We rented a big stone house set back from the road. It was high on a hill overlooking the casino and the ocean below. The rent was absurdly low. The landlord owned several homes and was fearful that the residences might be invaded by revolutionary forces during these troubled times. He was elated to have the house occupied. The house was cold at night, and there was no central heating. However, it was fully equipped in Portuguese upper class fashion; place settings with crystal wine and champagne service for 80 people. The full-time gardener made sure there were fresh flowers throughout the house daily. Most importantly to us, however, the family was now together seven days a week, a relief to Judy and me.

I commuted daily from Estoril to my office in Lisbon. Now, as 1975 began, my plans to open Kentucky Fried Chicken restaurants were stifled by the new government. They decreed that no equipment would be permitted to be imported from the United States, and no royalties could be sent to the U.S. Since both were critical to the Kentucky Fried Chicken operation, I couldn't open any outlets.

People had previously assumed that I was with the CIA; without any KFC business activity, they were now certain of it.

No one in Portugal would be enjoying Kentucky Fried Chicken any time soon. My weekdays were spent lining up potential locations for the restaurant chain when and if we were permitted to open. I developed compelling ad campaigns with our advertising agency, and I struck deals with suppliers, which would await an unknown future. I fought my stress by swimming laps at lunchtime in the Lisbon Sheraton pool and by working out in their gym.

Judy had obtained a teaching position at the American school in Lisbon and traveled each day with the girls to that American haven in an increasingly unfriendly country. About two thirds of the students were American; the remainder of the students were Canadian, Japanese, Taiwanese, Spanish, and a few Portuguese. While there were considerable numbers of Europeans in the city, nearly all their children attended Lisbon's British School.

Most of the parents of the American kids were attached to NATO or to the U.S. Embassy. However, several were listed as "missionaries," code for CIA personnel. No one took too seriously the claim that anyone really worked as a missionary in this Catholic country; there were not a lot of conversions or proselytizing opportunities.

The school provided an excellent education for Lynn and Liz. The curriculum was typically American, although everyone learned Portuguese, and the older children studied additional languages. Our two girls thrived on the exposure to different nationalities and lifestyles, the full range of sports and after school activities, and their growing familiarity with world politics.

When I would ask my daughters whether they were bothered by what was going on around them, their inevitable response was a laugh and "Não problema, papa." They were handling the situation just fine.

We continued to drive south to the Algarve on weekends. There was no place more beautiful than that province in the winter. The citrus scent of lemon, orange, and grapefruit trees was everywhere. Sweet-smelling almond blossoms blanketed the countryside in white. There is a fable that long ago an Algarve king married a Scandinavian princess; she became homesick for her native land, so the king planted a million almond trees to give her the illusion of snow in wintertime.

Beauty aside, our cherished life on this southern coast had changed. Roadblocks and searches were now a part of the driving experience, and our social life was no longer carefree. When our right-wing friends, Kiko and Francesca Cabral came to our house on Saturday nights, they were anxious to listen to the BBC news of the Portuguese situation on our short wave radio. They didn't trust the coverage from the Portuguese media, and they were fearful of being reported if they had a short-wave radio in their home.

We would go out for dinner as well with our left-wing friends, João and Luisa Cutilero. He was one of Portugal's most prominent sculptors. Their enthusiasm over what they considered the inevitable communist control of Portugal was disturbing to us, yet convincing.

I had realized long before that extremism on the left or the right is equally harmful and unacceptable. Portugal had traded one for the other, and, as a result, the country was still suffering. So were we.

By spring, the country was in a state of near anarchy. The communists held tightly onto power but were not able to secure more than 15% popular support in the polls. The Socialist Party obtained about 40% backing in the polls, but they did not have the organizational infrastructure or leadership qualities to run the country. Four other political parties divided the remainder of the support of the people.

In March, Judy, the girls, and I flew to Porto, Portugal's second largest city for the weekend. We were the guests of the Alves family, my business partners in the KFC venture. Three brothers ran the business, and before the Revolution, they were one of the wealthiest families in the country. As was true with most upper class Portuguese, their major holdings had been in the colonies, banana plantations in Mozambique and oil wells and coffee plantations in Angola. All that had disappeared now, and it was not looking as if Kentucky Fried Chicken would achieve any profits soon either. Nevertheless, the brothers and their wives were gracious hosts to the four of us, taking us to dinner on Saturday night to one of Porto's best restaurants.

After dinner, we returned to the huge home where we were staying, on the Alves estate. Lynn and Liz and the Alves kids were put to bed.

The adults sat around talking and consuming the city's most famous product, fine port. Suddenly, the quiet night was interrupted by gunshots in the distance. The brothers rushed out of the room and quickly returned with rifles that had materialized from somewhere. Each brother grabbed one and headed for the door. "The real revolution has come," one shouted, and they implored me to protect the women and children, as they went to war.

As it turned out, I didn't need to touch the gun they had left me. There was one person killed that night in Porto, not the first but the last of a handful of fatalities of the Portuguese Revolution. Lynn and Liz had slept through the gunfire.

After that evening, red carnations would once again be more representative than rifles of the country's events. Yet, that was the night we decided that this was not the right year for Judy and me to be bringing up our children in Portugal.

Liz and Lynn continued to say, "Não problema," when queried about their feelings, and it became a favorite phrase in our house. Nevertheless, in April, when Grey Advertising, with whom I had worked previously, informed me that they would like to hire me back, I accepted, on the condition that I could be employed in an international assignment. Our family had developed an insatiable appetite for foreign living. Grey agreed and we made plans to leave beautiful Portugal.

It was May 1st. Just before we were scheduled to depart from the country, we witnessed the May Day festivities. In many nations, the first of May is a Labor Day observance. In communist countries, however, it was much more, a fervent, almost fanatical celebration of communism. In Portugal, that year, the American Embassy suggested that Americans remain inside their homes for safety, and we complied. As we heard the sound of the bands and viewed the parades on television, we remembered how everything had begun for us exactly a year before. There was so much we would miss about the Portugal we loved, but it was time to go.

Some months later, Judy, Lynn, Liz, and I were living in Toronto, where Grey, true to its promise, had found me a position. So much was different from where we had been the previous year. Then, as the four of us were sitting around the television one night, we heard the news. "The Parti Quebecois, the P.Q., has won the election in Quebec and has vowed to make Quebec separate from Canada. Prime Minister Pierre Trudeau has said he will not allow it to happen. There could well be serious consequences for Canada."

Liz was the first to speak. "Não problema," she said.

Lynn and Liz at Algarve home

Liz is not intimidated by revolutionary graffiti

Separate Rooms

The flight attendant glided down the aisle, taking drink orders. "Would your wife care for a beverage?" she queried, referring to my seat companion, who was dozing.

"I don't really know," I responded. I didn't correct the stewardess' incorrect presumption of our marital status. She could be forgiven for not realizing that we were traveling from continent to continent hardly knowing one another. I had met Nicole only six days before.

I was the Director of Marketing of Norton Simon, Inc., one of the country's largest conglomerates. Our divisions included Hunt-Wesson Foods, Canada Dry Beverages, Avis Rent-A-Car, and McCall's and Redbook Magazines. We had chosen to expand into the cosmetic industry, and we had made a provisional deal to acquire Max Factor. It was privately owned, available for purchase, and we had leaped at the opportunity. We were entering the final twenty days of our due diligence examination of their company to assure ourselves that there were no unpleasant surprises. Their finances looked solid, and their U.S. operation was fine. I just needed to spend two weeks in Japan, Factor's second largest market, to ascertain that all was satisfactory there.

Although I was perfectly capable of evaluating Max Factor's marketing and advertising, I had no competency in judging the quality of their product line. Certainly, there was no one at Norton Simon with that kind of knowledge. It had not been easy to find someone with the cosmetic product expertise who could fly to Japan with me for a couple of weeks.

However, fortuitously, the Beauty Editor of Glamour Magazine had recently announced her retirement. The publisher had brought in an experienced editor to fill the vacancy, causing Nicole, the young, talented Associate Beauty Editor, to resign her position. The timing was perfect for me. Nicole was fully knowledgeable about cosmetic and skin care products, and she was available for my two-week assignment.

When I had interviewed Nicole the week before, it seemed to be an easy decision for each of us. I required her expertise, and she appeared to be interested in the well-paying project. Only at the end of the interview had there been any complication.

"The assignment sounds fascinating." She had hesitated a moment, then added, "Do I understand that you and I would be traveling together to Tokyo for two weeks?" She was pleasant but wary. "Alone?"

I nodded. "Yes. Would that be a problem?"

"I want you to know that I'm engaged," she said earnestly.

"Well, that makes us even," I said. "I'm married with two darling little daughters." It was technically correct, although my wife and I had been experiencing major marital problems, and we were planning to separate upon my return from Japan. I figured that I had better not mention any of that if I wanted Nicole to accept the assignment.

"Nicole, please don't worry. We have an important job to do here. This trip is about business."

She paused. " I would like to discuss it with my fiancé. May I give you a final answer tomorrow?"

I agreed.

The following morning, she had accepted. Over the next couple of days, I made arrangements and booked appointments in Japan. Now, we were in the sky, taking the long flight from New York to Tokyo.

"I'd love a Diet Coke," the sleepy voice next to me spoke. I had ordered a scotch, and we spent the next couple of hours getting to know each other.

Nicole had graduated from Vassar with a major in Art History. During the ten years since college, she had worked in Product Development and Product Management, first at Estée Lauder and then at Revlon before joining Glamour. She had not traveled since her junior year in college, which she had spent in Florence, Italy. The opportunity to see Japan was tremendously exciting, she told me.

I was incredulous. This extremely attractive, fashionable New Yorker had not traveled at all during the past ten years. She shopped at Bergdorf's and Henri Bendel, was familiar with the fine restaurants of Manhattan, and knew the city's museums and galleries intimately. Yet, she had very little exposure to the world.

"Why have you chosen to stay so close to home?" I asked her.

"Richard doesn't really enjoy travel," she replied.

"Richard is your fiancé, I assume. How long have you two been together?" I inquired.

"We've been engaged for eight years."

I had never heard of an eight-year engagement. I tried to not let my astonishment show. "How does that happen? Do you live together?" I asked gingerly.

"We see each other on weekends. He is a brilliant oncologist. He doesn't want to get married until he's fully established. What about you?" she parried my questions.

I told her about my career, in which I had alternated between the advertising agency world and client-side employment at marketing-oriented companies. I was only a few years older than she was, but I had been married for ten years. Now, the marriage was ending, but I didn't mention that to Nicole. I showed her photographs of my two daughters.

"What's your wife like?"

I described my wife, a lovely lady, a marvelous mother, and an avid and talented teacher in the suburbs. I commuted from our home in Westchester to work in New York City. I avoided telling Nicole how my wife and I had grown apart. Somehow, that would have seemed to contradict my original conversation with her. Perhaps she sensed my marital problems.

"I think loyalty is the most important thing between a man and a woman," Nicole said.

"More important than love?" I asked.

"Perhaps," she replied.

"I suspect you would add patience and perseverance to your attribute list," I rejoined, referring to her lengthy engagement.

She laughed. "Touché," she ended the conversation.

By the time we landed in Tokyo, we had discussed our upcoming schedules for the next two weeks. Nicole would be visiting Max Factor's Japanese manufacturing operation; she would be conducting store checks at the retailers that stocked their products; and she would be interviewing Japanese consumers to the extent that language permitted. I would be spending my time at the Max Factor offices and at their distributors and advertising agencies. We would each have full schedules.

Our plane touched down at Narita Airport. Nicole and I were tired, well-fed, and now good friends. Max Factor had sent two people to collect us and our bags and to escort us to our hotel. For the first time, it occurred to me how much they were determined that I enjoy this trip; the acquisition was very important to them.

We checked into the Hotel Okura. As I signed the registration form for our two rooms, the man behind the counter glanced quickly at

Nicole, then turned to me and said in a soft-spoken, dignified manner, "Perhaps you would prefer a larger, double room, sir."

I may have hesitated imperceptibly, but I remembered well what I had committed to Nicole at our very first meeting. "No, thank you. Separate rooms, please."

Our rooms were next to one another. We each unpacked, showered, changed, and then met to explore the hotel. This would be our home for the next two weeks, and we walked a bit outside to get some fresh air and to become oriented to the Roppongi district in which the hotel was located. It wasn't until we returned to our rooms that we discovered that there was a connecting door between the rooms.

"I thought that registration clerk had a gleam in his eye," Nicole said. By now, we were comfortable enough with one another to laugh at that unintended feature of our accommodations.

Exhausted, we were ready for sleep. We had appointments the next morning, Nicole at the Factor manufacturing facility, and I at their business offices. We made arrangements to have an early room service breakfast in my room. I wished her good night at her door.

"You could stay with me tonight, if you'd like," I said, half jokingly.

"This trip is about business," she reminded me. We shared a friendly hug.

At breakfast, we made plans to meet for dinner. Then, we caught taxis for our respective destinations.

During the next few days, I had one meeting after another. As was typical of so many international companies in Japan, Max Factor's senior positions were filled by Japanese executives and the middle management people were generally Americans. I spent time with each of them. I met also with the owners of the five distributor firms that were responsible for selling Max Factor products in Japan. Factor is truly an anomaly in Japan since it is one of only a few U.S. companies that were introduced into the country prior to World War II. As a result, it is a fixture in Japanese culture, more similar to Japanese beauty brands such as Shiseido and Kao than to more recent American arrivals such as Revlon.

Nicole was fully occupied as well. She spent her days talking to the production people, observing the manufacturing process, and reviewing samples of Max Factor's products, as well as those of their competitors.

There was one major unforeseen circumstance. Each of the Max Factor executives expected to entertain me during my stay. In their male-oriented business society, that meant I was required to spend every night socializing with men without their wives. When I once suggested that Nicole join us, the social rules of the Japanese business environment were explained to me: Nicole was no more welcome than were my hosts' wives.

To adjust to this situation, I developed an unusual schedule for each day. Nicole and I would begin the morning with room service breakfast in my room. Then we would depart for our business agendas. She and I would reconvene in the early evening and have dinner together in one of the Roppongi restaurants. I would usually begin with a scotch, and Nicole, always the non-drinker, would order a Coca Cola. We would share stories from the work day over robatayaki or kaiseki or sushi, finishing with the omnipresent green tea ice cream. We ended with her admonition to me to behave myself in the wicked city, as I kissed her good night at the door of her hotel room.

I wasn't pleased about indulging in two dinners each day, but I had little choice. Nicole needed to be fed, and I couldn't insult my Japanese hosts by declining their invitations. After leaving Nicole, I would proceed to the lobby, meet my evening's host and begin that night's socializing. We would inevitably dine at a fancy restaurant and follow with the customary drinking at a hostess bar, or, one time, at a fabled geisha bar. After a particularly heavy round of drinking one night, I was taken to a sento, a public bath, for what my host assured me was the perfect antidote to any potential hangover, a bath administered by an attractive young lady, culminating in her blow-drying and styling my hair while I was in the tub.

Each morning, I would describe the previous night's activities to Nicole over breakfast. She usually entered my room through the interior door, and most often her breakfast attire was the hotel-supplied white terrycloth robe, wrapped tightly around her. Our relationship had evolved to the point where seeing one another at breakfast and dinner was the best part of the day. However, the ground rules had been established, and morning and evening hugs and kisses were the extent of our physical relationship.

At the end of the first week, I had planned a surprise for Nicole. Since we had no business scheduled over the weekend, I had arranged a three-day sightseeing trip. Late Friday afternoon, we boarded the bullet train from Tokyo to Kyoto. The train rushed through the Japanese countryside, allowing us a glimpse of the majestic Mt. Fuji in the distance.

Nicole was thrilled by the train trip. She had enjoyed Tokyo, despite the obligatory early endings to her evenings. Now, she was traveling through Japan to Kyoto, the country's greatest treasure.

"This is extraordinary; I've never known anything like it, you know," Nicole said as we pulled into the Shin-Osaka station, a twenty-minute taxi ride from Kyoto.

"I'm glad." I had been feeling guilty all week about my socializing while she was confined to her hotel room. I wanted desperately to please this lovely, attractive woman.

As the taxi arrived at our hotel, I turned to Nicole, "I suppose you would like us to have separate rooms here too." I had booked two rooms, but I had not mentioned that to her.

Her voice was soft. "I really think we should. It's what loyalty and commitment are all about."

For the next three days, we filled every available hour with viewing the attractions of the area; the stunning Kiyomizu and Heian Shrines; the glorious Kinkakuji and Ryoanji Temples; Kyoto's Imperial Palace; the Nijo Castle; and a side trip to Nara, where we strolled through Nara Park and fed the deer. During the evenings, we dined leisurely, free from our weekday constraints of early, rushed dinners. We had experienced Kyoto's beautiful sights, breathtaking architecture and gardens, and absorbed so much Japanese history.

Our train carried us back to Tokyo late Monday afternoon. "I never thought I would love a place as much as Florence," Nicole said. She sipped her Coca Cola and turned to me. "You really know how to make a lady happy."

"It's not me, it's the Coke," I teased. I was feeling pretty pleased too.

We had four more days of intensive work in Tokyo. Nicole spent much of her time in the city's enormous department stores, Isetan, Matsuya, Tobu, and Seibu. She interviewed the incredibly polite women and girls who were customers in the stores about their opinion of Factor's cosmetic and skin care products. I visited J. Walter Thompson and McCann-Erickson, Max Factor's advertising agencies. I met also with the people at A.C. Nielsen, the research and retail audit company, to confirm the Factor market share.

By the following Friday, we had completed our work. It had been an intense and thorough analysis. At the end of the day, Nicole and I said our final farewells to our respective Max Factor contacts, as the hotel's secretarial staff typed Nicole's report to me.

On Saturday, I packed my things, including the silk kimonos I had purchased for my wife and daughters. Nicole and I taxied to the airport, boarded our plane, and flew toward home.

Seated, we discussed our enthusiasm for the Max Factor Japanese operation. There would be no doubt that it would be a valuable part of Norton Simon. For some reason, the flight of more than twelve hours seemed particularly short. Perhaps it was our gaining the extra day; flying over, we had lost a day to the International Date Line, and now we were given it back. More likely, it was the ease with which Nicole and I related. This woman, to whom I had been so attracted for two weeks, was now a friend. She had not only done an outstanding job on the business assignment, but she had taught me so much about loyalty and commitment. I would give my marriage another fervent try.

I reached into my briefcase, and extracted the souvenir I had intended for Nicole. I gave her the coke bottle I had been carrying. It was covered with Japanese characters. "Just one of a hundred you emptied," I told her.

As we landed, she handed me a wrapped gift. After unwrapping it, I found an art book titled, "Japanese Erotic Prints Through The Centuries." The enclosed card was inscribed to me, "The one area not covered on this trip."

She touched my arm. "Thank you for the experience of my life. Let me know what happens with Factor."

I assured her I would.

I caught only a glimpse of Richard's back at the airport before I met my wife with an embrace. That night, I told her that I thought we should give our marriage another chance. We had made a commitment to one another, I said, and we should find a way to make it work.

The middle of the next week, the President of Norton Simon, the Director of Finance, and I presented our purchase recommendation to the Board of Directors. The Board approved it, and a month later, Max Factor became a new division of our company.

After the Board presentation, I wandered back to my office, and, as I accessed my phone mail messages in habitual fashion, I heard the familiar voice: Nicole. I listened carefully.

"It was an incredible trip. I learned so much from you, most importantly about myself. I broke up last night with Richard, something I should have done long ago. I hope you call me, but please call only if you are interested in a serious relationship with me."

I took a deep breath as I looked toward the telephone. I sat for a couple of minutes. Then, I headed out the door of my office and made my way to the commuter train. My wife and I were to have dinner that night, as we began our reconciliation effort.

New York is a big city, and I lost track of what happened to Nicole. That doesn't mean I never wondered.

Author visits Kyoto temple

Invitation to Hollywood

It was just after dawn as I exited the taxi. The frosty December air blew into my face from across Lake Ontario. I was arriving at the downtown Toronto production facilities of the giant CBC television network. I was to appear for a televised interview by the host of the morning show, which would be viewed broadly throughout Canada. The interview was to take the form of an adversarial interchange between me and a lawyer named David Himelfarb, who represented James Cagney.

Hollywood has never known a bigger success story than that of James Cagney. The son of an Irish bartender and a Norwegian mother was born in 1899 in New York City. He grew up on the Lower East Side and helped support his family as a waiter and poolroom racker, among other occupations. To supplement his income, he joined a revue as a female impersonator. In 1920, he was in the chorus of the Broadway production, "Pitter Patter," and after touring in vaudeville with his wife, Frances, he began playing leads on Broadway in 1925. Following the success of "Penny Arcade," he was brought to Hollywood in 1920 with co-star, Joan Blondell, to appear in the film version of the show, renamed "Sinners' Holiday."

Signed by Warner Brothers, Cagney became a star within a year on the strength of his performance in "The Public Enemy," as a ruthless Prohibition gangster, who, in a memorable scene, smashes a grapefruit into the face of a gang girlfriend. This presaged the cocky, pugnacious characters he would portray in subsequent films. An atypical Hollywood star, he was short and ordinary-looking, but his

83

ebullient energy and aggressive personality made him the ideal lead for the gangster films and the social dramas of the Depression era. Later, he proved his acting versatility by playing such diverse roles as Bottom in "A Midsummer's Night Dream" and George M. Cohan in "Yankee Doodle Dandy," in which he sang and danced and for which he won an Oscar as Best Actor. By 1939, Cagney was Warner Brothers' highest paid star. In 1974, he became the first actor to receive the Life Achievement Award of the American Film Institute, and, in 1980, he was similarly honored by Washington's Kennedy Center. In 1984, he was decorated with the Medal of Freedom, the U.S. government's highest civilian award.

If James Cagney reached the pinnacle in Hollywood, Mae Clark's career was spent on the bumpy moguls of the road to film fame. She was born in 1907, the daughter of a motion picture organist. She began as a cabaret dancer at age 16 and soon played supporting roles in stage musicals and dramas. She made her film debut in 1929 and for several years was a successful leading lady. She suffered through three failed marriages, and by the late 1930's, her career was in decline. Thereafter, she was reduced to bit parts.

Mae Clarke's only role for which she is well-remembered was one of her smaller ones, as the mob moll who was the recipient of the grapefruit pushed in her face by James Cagney in the movie classic, "The Public Enemy." Her look of horror was genuine as the grapefruit hit her face in what would become a famous movie poster; Cagney had assured her in rehearsal that he would fake the maneuver.

During the final years of James Cagney's career, I was an American living in Toronto. I was the President and CEO of the Canadian arm of a large, international advertising agency, Grey Advertising. We created, produced, and ran advertising for multinational companies such as Clairol, Avis, General Foods, Playtex, Revlon, Procter & Gamble, Timex and Canon. For these esteemed clients, we would use the advertising developed in the United States, perhaps with modest changes to adapt to the needs of the Canadian marketplace.

Our creative people, copywriters, art directors, and television producers worked on these adaptations faithfully, if without over-whelming enthusiasm. Their real excitement came when they developed advertising for local clients, those that were not assigned to us internationally. For these local clients, there were no constraints from abroad, and the creative juices could flow. Great advertising campaigns were developed, therefore, for a major Canadian bank, an airline, a television station, a restaurant chain, and so on.

The year was 1985. We had recently received an assignment from the Airwick Corporation to create advertising for one of their products, Binaca Breath Spray. The good news for our creative people was that they would have the opportunity to develop the advertising without any need to adapt it from elsewhere. The challenge was that the product was small in importance and tiny in size. It was a slim metal spray tube, slightly thicker than a fountain pen and not nearly as long. After removing the cap, the user sprayed a small dose of scented freshener into his or her mouth. The product's inconspicuousness made it easily portable. This was not an airline or a bank; it was hardly a necessity in anyone's life.

Our creative department went to work. A young art director and an even younger writer were given the assignment to make Binaca Breath Spray somehow important. When they completed the task, a truly brilliant advertising campaign had been developed.

The writer and art director team knew that, under Canadian law, copyrights expire after fifty years. So, they used famous old movie stills from the early 1930's to develop dramatic transit posters. The oversized King Kong with a helpless maiden in his grasp was combined with the headline, "Bad breath can be an enormous prob-lem." The frightening shot of Dracula was married to the headline, "Bad breath can be a scary situation." Finally, there was James Cagney in the most famous scene from "The Public Enemy," mashing a grapefruit into Mae Clarke's face at the breakfast table with the understated headline, "Bad breath can upset your morning."

Combined with a secondary line, "Fortunately, fresh breath is a spray away," and a picture of the tiny Binaca spray canister, the ads were produced in stark black and white. They were immediately a great success. People on the subways and buses didn't know whether to cringe or giggle at the large, graphic visuals with the solution being a spray of Binaca. The creative team had done a marvelous job, and the product began selling exceptionally well.

I was a pleased advertising executive. My company was the fastest growing agency in the country, and we had just received the latest of several awards for the Binaca campaign. But, when I opened my mail one day in November of 1985, I found a legal document, informing me that James Cagney was suing Airwick, Grey Advertising, and me personally for our Binaca advertising. In case the shock of the lawsuit had not had its full effect, I had only to read that day's Toronto Star, the city's afternoon newspaper. In a blazing headline, the Star informed readers that Cagney was suing us for $1,000,000.00 U. S. dollars, which converted to $1,400,000.00 Canadian, the largest lawsuit of its kind at that time in Canadian history.

The legal action was rather technical. Because the copyright for the movies and the movie stills had expired, they were in the public domain, and there was no reason why we couldn't use them. However, James Cagney was feeling denigrated by being associated with a mouth spray and he claimed that he was being exploited. He was on extremely questionable legal ground, but I was nonetheless gasping over the huge lawsuit.

Over the next few weeks, articles about the legal action appeared regularly in the Canadian newspapers. They were often accompanied by photographs of the advertisement, so, if Cagney was unhappy about an association with breath spray, his lawsuit was hardly helping his cause. However, Airwick and Grey were enjoying the publicity immensely.

Cagney's lawyer, David Himelfarb, was relishing the chance to be in the media. "We're not talking copyright here. James Cagney has the right to exploit his face, and he hasn't granted it to anyone. It'd be different if he granted it to Grey Advertising and said that you can use my face to sell your product. But he hasn't. Never would. And never will," Himelfarb postured.

I countered in the newspapers. "The copyright has expired. We have every right to use the movie stills. We never suggested that James Cagney was endorsing Binaca."

The legal battle was also being covered in the U.S. On December 17th, the Wall Street Journal ran a long article about it, making fun of Cagney. Public opinion was definitely turning in our favor.

The next day was when Himelfarb and I arrived at the CBC Network's studios for our early morning television session. The interview and debate went well with sparks flying between us and Binaca receiving prominent publicity.

Upon leaving the television studio, David Himelfarb approached me. "May I buy you some breakfast," he asked.

I was startled. Regaining my composure, I responded, "As long as there's no grapefruit."

Over coffee and toast, he began. "Mr. Cagney is furious at you."

I had visions of the gangsters that James Cagney played in so many of his movies coming after me. The fact that he was well into his eighties didn't occur to me just then.

Himelfarb continued. "Nevertheless, he thinks this might be the right time for you and him to come to a settlement."

By the time we had finished our eggs, we had worked out a deal. I would fly to Los Angeles, make a public apology to James Cagney and hand him a check for $1,000.00. Cagney would say a few words to the assembled media.

"Of course, the amount of the check should not be disclosed," Himelfarb said to me with a smile. I understood. The million dollar lawsuit had become a mere thousand dollars, a fact that would not be in James Cagney's interest to publicize.

"I think I could agree to that," I offered after a moment. I was thrilled. Airwick would be more than happy to pay the $1,000.00, the value of a few hours' sales of Binaca. I would have the opportunity to meet with and to talk to one of the great film stars of all time.

Himelfarb said that he would finalize the details with Cagney and would be back to me later in the day.

When I heard from him in the afternoon, Himelfarb told me that Cagney wanted to make one modification. Mae Clarke was now in a nursing home and could use the money. After I was to make my apology speech, Cagney would announce to the reporters present that he would be endorsing my check to the account of Mae Clarke.

The press conference was arranged for noon on Christmas Eve in Los Angeles. I would fly there the day before and would return on the redeye flight Christmas Eve. I would be home for Christmas with my family.

I worked on my apology speech: very respectful toward James Cagney; a few humorous allusions to the lawsuit; and a nod to the virtues of Binaca Breath Spray. I thought I had captured the essence of the event.

However, a few days before Christmas, James Cagney, in failing health, was admitted to the hospital. Our ceremony was cancelled, and he was not to recover. In early 1986, the legendary film star died. By that time, our check had been paid to him.

Shortly after Cagney's death, I received a letter from Mae Clarke. She had heard that I had made a "large payment" to James Cagney, and she was inquiring as to whether I might be able to send her something as well. She noted that she needed the money considerably more than James Cagney did, a rather indisputable fact. I replied, informing her that the Cagney estate had received a payment that was intended for her and that she should contact them. I later heard back from her that she was extremely pleased and appreciative with how the matter was resolved.

Mae Clarke died in 1992, living almost as long as had James Cagney. When he died, there was worldwide attention. Upon her death, there was minimal media reporting. While I had met neither, they had become for me much more then "The Public Enemy." From a distance, I briefly had joined them in their world.

Articles from Toronto Star and The Wall Street Journal

Soul Mates

Walking briskly, I covered the short distance from my apartment on Wellesley Street to the Sutton Place Hotel's restaurant. I didn't want to be late for my breakfast.

Recently, I had become divorced. Since separating from my wife, I had experienced the typical confusion of those in my situation who had married young, enthusiasm about my new freedom, alternating with loneliness and a need for connection.

Head of an advertising agency, my job allowed me to meet a multitude of desirable women, and I had taken full advantage. During the past two years, I had dated several prominent women, a top model, a high-powered entertainment lawyer, a TV news anchor, and an opera diva. None of my flings had been fully satisfying, and I felt the need for something more.

I was to begin my day with breakfast at the Sutton Place's Sanssouci restaurant, my usual spot. It was a perfect location for me, just a long stone's throw from my apartment and a couple of blocks from there to my office. Usually, I ate with a client or an agency colleague. That morning, however, I had a breakfast date with an attractive blonde who was another morning regular at Sanssouci. Over the past few weeks, we had exchanged greetings of "good morning," and the previous Friday, I had introduced myself and suggested we have breakfast sometime. She had asked for my business card and had said she would call. She had telephoned my office later that morning and had scheduled the breakfast with Angie, my secretary.

93

My interest in having breakfast with Jennifer Ross was simple: She was the best-looking woman I had seen in some time. Added to that, I found it fascinating to see this seemingly single woman at 7:30 or 8:00 every morning, either dining alone or with one or more companions, but always there. Why?

Our breakfast answered the question. She had separated from her husband a month before. She had breakfast daily at the Sanssouci restaurant because she lived at the Sutton Place Hotel in an apartment on one of the hotel's upper floors.

Jennifer was the producer and on-screen personality in a new television show which would be launched in September. She was the mother of two young children, a nine year old girl and a boy who was seven. Her weekends were spent at a farm north of the city with her kids, who were staying there with her husband.

I told Jennifer about my life. She knew quite a lot about my advertising agency, not surprising, given that she was in the television business. I expressed my pride in my two daughters and told her about them. The breakfast had to be cut short because I had considerable work to do that morning. It was a busy and exciting day for me as I was scheduled to be a head table guest at a cocktail reception and luncheon with former President Jimmy Carter.

I had enjoyed the breakfast and looked forward to seeing this stunning woman again; she appeared to juggle motherhood and a demanding career effortlessly. We arranged another breakfast for the following week.

Over the next couple of months, we had breakfast on a few more weekday mornings. My work was keeping me busy, and Jennifer was intensely involved in preparations for her new television show. In late June, we had dinner together on a Wednesday night. We talked in detail about Jennifer, her marriage, her husband, Nick, and about her kids. She told me how she missed the children, who were at the farm she had purchased in a last ditch effort to salvage her marriage.

Jennifer shared with me details about what sounded like a terrible marriage. Nick beat her; he was always stoned from cocaine; his father was an alcoholic, and Nick grew up as a street fighter. He was a loser who could never be successful in anything, and he was abusive to the kids. Jennifer lived for the weekends, when Nick would leave the farm so that she could spend time with the children.

"You really should get rid of that guy," I told her, after hearing the story.

"I'm beginning to think you're right," she replied. "I've tried to keep it together for the kids, but it makes less and less sense to me. One day I will meet my soul mate and then move on."

During that period, I was in a full-time relationship with Beth. That is, I was in as full-time a relationship as one could with a woman who lived in another city an hour's flight away. Beth would fly in for three-day weekends with me every week either in the city or at my country house in Vermont. The relationship seemed to be evolving well, and Beth was beginning to leave her clothes at one or another of my homes.

In July, Beth and I went to Vermont for a ten-day vacation. We had a lovely time bicycling, canoeing, playing tennis, relaxing and enjoying ourselves. It could have been the precursor for our becoming engaged. Except for one thing: Near the end of our time there, I received a call from Jennifer. She apologized for disturbing me on vacation, but she "wanted to say hello," and was "looking forward to our getting together" after my return. Perhaps, I wasn't quite ready to get engaged, I told Beth. I was astounded and flattered that Jennifer had found a way to track me down in Vermont. I looked forward to seeing her.

I returned from vacation to find a bottle of my favorite Spanish wine at my apartment building's reception desk, a gift from Jennifer. The attached note asked me to call her. The die was cast. I told Beth over the telephone that I wasn't ready for the relationship to become more serious, and we ended it.

In early August, Jennifer invited me to spend a Saturday with her and her kids at the farm. I arrived to the aroma of bran muffins baking in the oven, several horses in the pasture adjoining the stable, and as bucolic an environment as could be imagined two hours' drive from the city. Jennifer's kids were cute. Jill was, if possible, prettier than Jennifer, and Rickie was a bundle of energy. There was little furniture, but Nick's clothes and belongings were everywhere. I wondered where he might be.

I was impressed. She was a woman who was comfortable in the world of business, who was a television producer and performer, who was an active, involved mother of two nice kids. In addition, she seemed at home in a farm kitchen. I was falling for her.

Jennifer and I spent the next weekend in Vermont. We enjoyed an idyllic three days, making love by the fire, soaking in the hot tub by candlelight, and taking night walks under the full moon. We fell in love and talked of a life together.

As we were hiking the nature trail at the Southern Vermont Art Center, Jennifer said, "There's one thing I want to tell you." She sounded somber. We stopped, and she talked. She told me about a charge of credit card fraud against Nick and her. She had played a minor role, and Nick had gone to jail for nine months. Apparently, a sergeant in the police force had been "out to get Nick since his wild teenage days and used the charge to finally land him." I was stunned by what I was hearing, but Jennifer's sincerity, her forthrightness, and my feeling for her mitigated against a stronger reaction.

In the weeks before, Jennifer had told me how much she wanted to leave Nick. Now, she expressed to me how deeply she wanted me.

"But you should have a period of dating after a ten-year marriage," I pointed out to her.

Jennifer said that she and Nick had separated four times now, and each time she had returned just for the kids. She wasn't "into dating," didn't need it, "and finally was finished with trying to save the marriage." She was sure of her feelings.

Jennifer took my hand. "I've met my soul mate," she told me with tears in her eyes.

Jennifer was convincing, especially, of course, to me who was happy to be convinced. After all, this was the woman for whom I had ended my relationship with Beth.

In late August, Jennifer and Jill moved into my apartment. Rickie was staying at the farm with Nick. The move was logistically simple; Jennifer had no furniture or possessions, only clothes and cosmetics, one or two pictures, and a vase. She commented that she had tried to buy some furniture the previous month, but the store had turned down her credit card because it had exceeded its limit. I would hear that explanation countless times in the future, necessitating me to open my checkbook regularly.

Jennifer's weekly television program, "The Ross Report," was launched in September. She interviewed celebrities across the broad spectrum of entertainment, the arts, education, and business. As well, Jennifer would dispense her strongly-held opinions against junk foods and sugar, guns, sexual freedom, and liberal child-raising. Her show quickly became immensely popular. Viewers regularly approached us in restaurants to thank her for her moral stands and to request autographs. Celebrities lined up to appear on her show. Jennifer's interviewing skill, conservative values, and classic beauty all combined to create star status for her and high ratings for the show.

One day in early October, Jennifer asked me if we could become engaged. She said that she was embarrassed to admit to her parents that she was living with me without a ring. Later that month, I presented her with a magnificent diamond engagement ring; she was pleased.

Jennifer wanted us to move into a house. She said that Nick would allow Rickie to join us if we had a nice home with enough room for the children to play. "You know how much it would mean to me to have Rickie as a part of our life. He's become so used to the farm, where he has all that space. We really need a bigger place."

What Jennifer said made sense. I had a feeling that we were moving too fast, but Jennifer was adamant about our needing a house. My compromise was that we would rent rather than buy. Over the next two weeks, we looked at houses all over the city and suburbs. Nothing was quite right for Jennifer until we discovered a newly-renovated five bedroom house on a quiet street in Rosedale.

The rent was outrageously expensive, but it was a beautiful house and only a five minute walk to the school for the kids. I signed a two-year lease. By the end of November, I had become expert at shopping for fine furniture, and the house's twelve rooms were fully furnished.

My advertising work was going well. I was finding my volunteer position as Chairman of the Board of the City's Children's Aid Society extremely satisfying. Jennifer was kept occupied with "The Ross Report," sometimes so busy that she would not arrive home until midnight.

The relationship had changed. Our lives seemed to intersect now only occasionally. I met alone with Jill's teacher; Jennifer was busy that night. I never had meals any more with the woman who was wearing my engagement ring. I was becoming nervous about the expenses, all of which were borne by me. So, when Jennifer asked me for $25,000.00 for "The Ross Report" "just until the network pays me the money it owes me," I said no.

Two days later, I pursued my usual Tuesday extended agenda. I left early for work and, at the end of the day, went directly to a Children's Aid Society meeting. When I arrived home, it was after 10 PM. I unlocked the front door and entered a ghost house.

There was no one inside. Even more shocking was that there was not a piece of furniture in the entire house; everything had been removed. I turned on the lights in the kitchen and in each bathroom and switched on the dining room chandelier. I walked through the huge house and found only my clothes and a few of my possessions. Even my file cabinet with my personal papers had been taken.

I was in a state of shock. I took a few deep breaths and headed for a bathroom. I was dizzy and needed to sit down. A toilet was the only seating option in the house. After considering my situation for a few moments, I made my way out of the house and got into my car. I parked the car in front of the house, opened the window a little, turned on the heat, and sat until morning.

I didn't bother to shave or change my clothes on Wednesday. I called my office and told Angie that I wouldn't be in that day. "I'm fine, Angie, I just need a day off. Please cancel my appointments."

I reached Jennifer at the television network's offices. "What's going on," I asked.

"Nick will be meeting with you," was her reply.

"Nick!" I exclaimed. "I don't want to meet with Nick."

"It's not about what you want," she said. "He'll see you at Sanssouci for a late breakfast in one hour. I think you know where it is." There was a click. She had hung up.

I had met Nick once before, when he had brought Rickie to the house. Then, I just disliked him. Now, I had to sit down with a man whom I despised.

We sat across from one another. The waiter came to the table, and I waved him away.

I let Nick talk first. His speech was prepared. "If you are wearing a recording device, it will not do you any good. I will not say anything that will be helpful to you. You are a pornographer and an alcoholic. You are a cocaine addict. Twice, when you were stoned on cocaine, you came home and abused my children in horrible ways. You are a menace, and you have taken advantage of my loving family. I will be easy on you: either you pay Jennifer the $25,000.00 that you owe her, and you pay the rest of the rent on the two-year lease on what is to be our house in Rosedale, or we will sue you for these things, and we will reveal your true nature to your advertising clients and to the Children's Aid Society. We hope for your sake that you make the right decision."

"No one would believe the nonsense you're spouting," I said, but my heart was pounding. Things like this didn't happen in real life, only in fiction.

"You'd be surprised what people will believe. Especially when it's true," he added, probably still thinking that I might be recording him.

"Is Jennifer in on your scheme," I asked. As my thoughts raced back to things she had said and done, I realized that, of course, she was. I was hurt, angry, and scared, all at the same time.

He took the offensive once again. "This is not a scheme. And, if you go near my wife or children again, I will knock you through the wall."

His face had turned from cool to cruel, and I suspected that his real personality was as much the nasty street fighter as the polished extorter.

"Well, what's your answer, pervert," he asked.

I was frightened and I felt helpless, but something led me to make a decision: It might cost me my career and my reputation, but I would not give in to this scum; somehow, I would fight.

"I need some time to make up my mind. I'll be back to Jennifer and you soon." I arose to go.

As I left the restaurant, I ran into someone I knew. He spoke to me excitedly. "I caught Jennifer's show the other day. She sure is an impressive lady."

"Yeah," I said. "Thanks."

I moved in with a friend and spent the next couple of days trying to figure out what to do. I met with several lawyers. Each suggested that I not fight Nick and Jennifer.

"Settling with them will be cheaper, you won't be slandered, and you'll be able to get on with your life," the lawyers said, as they proposed settlement wording.

They may have been right logically, but I saw it differently. If I didn't fight this, I would lose the diamond ring, the furniture, $25,000 and I would be paying Nick and Jennifer's rent. The financial cost was more than I could afford. Even more importantly, I had a stubborn determination to fight back and not give in to them.

I had thought through the sequence of events and had concluded that Jennifer and Nick had planned this many months ago. That suggested to me that it was likely that they had pursued similar schemes previously.

Fighting off my embarrassment, I began telling everyone what Nick and Jennifer had done and of what they had accused me. If I told people first, I believed it would lessen the effect of the tales they might hear from Nick and Jennifer. From friends, I obtained the name of a lawyer who was a fighter, and I hired him. The biggest thing I did, however, was to engage an outstanding private investigator; perhaps there might be previous criminal history, I figured, remembering the credit card fraud Jennifer had mentioned in Vermont.

Tom Crowley had originally been a police detective but had resigned from the police force and opened his own investigative operation to increase his earnings and to have predictable hours. He told me later that he had sacrificed the excitement of police work when he became a private investigator, but he recovered much of that excitement when he became involved in this case.

While I was stalling Nick from following through with his threats, I was pressuring Tom Crowley to complete his investigation quickly. Actually, he didn't need much pressure. He had never enjoyed a project more.

When three week later, Tom reported his findings to me, we both were stunned.

Ten years before, Nick and Jennifer had begun a trail of name and address changes that made my head spin. Nick Robinson had swept into Fenellon Falls, Ontario, a nondescript farm community and gained the attention of a pretty high school senior. When she graduated a month later, Mary Jo Prentice was happy to shed her farm origins and leave town with him. Leaving behind a trail of cons and scams across the United States and Canada, they had eventually become Nick and Jennifer Ross.

Their fraudulent activities demonstrated creativity and variety.

Jennifer had checked into a large suite in an upscale urban hotel. She negotiated a deal with the hotel's general manager. She would conduct a three-day women's issues symposium in the hotel's convention facilities and would split the proceeds with the hotel.

The hotel need cover only the advertising and publicity expenses and the food and beverage costs. The event was a success, raising considerable money, which was paid directly to Jennifer. She checked out of the hotel immediately after the symposium, accompanied by a man of Nick's description. When the hotel at checkout requested its share of the money, Jennifer flew into a rage over what she claimed had been attempted sexual assault by the hotel's general manager. She threatened to press charges against the hotel and manager if they harassed her for their money. The hotel declined the police request to charge her.

Jennifer and Nick had been accused by the police and postal authorities of fraud in their offering of a multiple video set of the Bible. The first 500 devotees who sent in $300.00 were to receive a magnificent 20 video version of the Bible. The videos were advertised in Christian magazines as "an opportunity for families to share the greatest book ever written together in front of the family television." The videos were never produced, and tens of thousands of dollars fleeced from the religious were not recovered.

Both Nick and Jennifer had been convicted of credit card fraud. They had arranged with a confederate to take their credit card and make major purchases with it before they reported the card lost. Nick had served time in prison, and Jennifer had been given probation based upon her pleading the need to look after her children. With Nick having received early release from jail, both were currently vulnerable to probation violation charges.

Tom Crowley told me he had more, but I couldn't wait. I had enough for now on these two characters. Armed with the investigative report, my lawyer arranged to obtain a search warrant from a judge, and the furniture was discovered at the farm. There were no bran muffins baking in the oven as I arrived with the police to identify my furniture.

It was a sad meeting when, on a rainy morning the next week, my lawyer and I met with Jennifer and her lawyer. Nick didn't show up. The four of us agreed quickly that Jennifer, the former Mary Jo Prentice, would return the diamond engagement ring and the furniture, and I would not press charges. I told her, much to my lawyer's surprise, that she could keep all the furniture I had purchased for Jill and Rickie's rooms. I felt so sorry for those two kids; the least I could do was to make sure they didn't lose their familiar bedrooms.

Jennifer wore no makeup that day. She had been crying. For the first time, I thought she looked unattractive.

Her assertiveness was also gone. She spoke quietly. "You know, I've lost the television show. Because of all the things you've said about me, I have to leave town."

"You've been through that before," I reminded her. "Just one question. Why did you ever tell me about the credit card fraud that day in Vermont?"

"I thought those days were over," she said, her eyes averted from mine.

"I don't believe that," I snapped.

"Anyway, you would have learned about that somehow and I wanted you to hear it from me," she added.

That was more likely the real reason. Over time, I have discovered that one characteristic of con artists is that they deflect issues by seemingly confronting them.

She looked at me for the first time since she had arrived at the meeting. "Things might have been different between us if I had met you before I met Nick."

I didn't bite. "No, Jennifer, when Nick Robinson arrived in Fenellon Falls and met Mary Jo Prentice, he found his soul mate."

By the time I exited the building, the rain had stopped. The sun was peeking through the clouds. I was looking forward to seeing my daughters that weekend for some real family time.

Author listens to President Carter's viewpoint

Author presents viewpoint to President Reagan

The Star Spangled
Serengeti

Ironically, my wife, Joanne and I live on a Vermont ski mountain, near the village of Manchester. I say "ironically" because, while we love Vermont, we have no interest at all in the icy temperatures and snowy roads of wintertime, much less in skiing. We enjoy spring's green rolling hills and profusion of wild flowers. We cherish our summer activities, golf, tennis, theatre and lawn concerts. We thrive on the blazing colors of the September and October foliage season. However, after the holidays are celebrated and the autumn chill has evolved to winter freeze, we can't wait to get away. By then, we are always anxious to trade our tranquil country life for an experience elsewhere, somewhere where it is warm.

After retiring to Vermont, we developed our own technique for exploring the world. We would choose a continent, book a month's rental in a condo or apartment, and then plan side trips, tours and independent travel in the area. All in all, we would spend thirteen weeks away, typically from February 1st to May 1st. In 1999, our rental was in Lagos, in Portugal's Algarve region and we traveled throughout Portugal, Spain, Morocco, and France. In 2000, our condo was located in the marina area of Puerto Vallarta, Mexico, and we walked in Belize, sailed among the Galapagos Islands, visited Quito, Ecuador, and explored Mexico. In 2001, we rented an apartment in Manly, the beach suburb of Sydney, and we commuted daily by ferry into the city past the glorious opera house. As well as Sydney, we explored most of the rest of Australia, hiked in both of

New Zealand's picture postcard islands and enjoyed a sybaritic week at a resort in Fiji. Each of our trips was a wonderful adventure.

By 2002, the world had changed. The events of September 11th forced a fearsome reality upon us all. Air travel was no longer merely transportation; it now seemed to be a frightening gamble. For most of our citizens, American flags and constant concern replaced exotic trips and carefree ways. Closer to home, both of our daughters were living in Manhattan with their husbands and babies. One of the families lived in Battery Park City, a stone's throw from the World Trade Center at the time of the plane crashes, and they had experienced a harrowing day; their apartment building had been rendered unlivable and they had been forced to retreat to a new home in northern Westchester.

Nevertheless, Joanne and I resolved to continue with our 2002 winter travel. We were mightily affected by the new paradigm of a world with terrorism, but our plans were made, and now, of course there was potential harm at home as well as in the rest of the world. I glibly told family and friends who suggested that we might want to reconsider our trip that we were more afraid of Vermont winters than of other dangers.

So, in early February, we were driven from our home on Bromley Mountain to Boston, where we outlasted the security checks at Logan Airport and boarded our American Airlines flight to London. Our final destination was Cape Town, and we would be in Africa for a total of three months. During our four weeks in Cape Town, our life included sightseeing, shopping, tennis, and golf on a windy links course with a glorious view across the bay to Table Mountain, excellent food and surprisingly good South African wine. Costs were at outrageously attractive prices, thanks to the exchange rate between the dollar and the rand. Our lengthy stay afforded us opportunities to visit the Langa township, where blacks live in conditions ranging from abject poverty to a borderline living standard; a tour of Robben Island, where Nelson Mandela spent eighteen years in prison; and a rewarding afternoon in the gallery of the National Assembly, the federal legislature, watching a frustrating debate on South Africa's biggest problem, AIDS. Cape Town was fascinating, and it was almost eerie to be in such an exciting city, packed with tourists, and yet to see so few Americans. September 11th had certainly taken its toll.

During the remainder of our time in Africa, we traveled around the continent, spending time in Zimbabwe, Zambia, Botswana, Namibia, Kenya, and Tanzania. We viewed a broad cross-section of southern Africa. It is difficult for us Americans to accept the fact that there are 53 countries in Africa (at last count), more than the total number of nations in Europe and North America combined. The countries' borders often owe more to colonial exigencies than to indigenous considerations, and their problems are immense. Beautiful Botswana has an AIDS epidemic even greater than that of South Africa, with over a third of the adult population afflicted. Kenya has spiraled downward with corruption and government ineptitude causing complete cynicism throughout the population. Perhaps most tragic in this part of the continent is Zimbabwe, where President Robert Mugagwe has cruelly and outrageously pandered to racial fears and mistrusts, virtually bringing the country to the edge of starvation. Joanne and I disregarded the warning against non-essential travel to Zimbabwe issued by our State Department. We weren't in danger; the citizens of Zimbabwe were.

For every problem or issue we witnessed in Africa, we were compensated by being the recipients of countless joys and kindnesses: the Kenyan taxi driver who turned off his meter to drive us to the site of the American Embassy bombing in Nairobi; the Muslim tour guide who, after escorting us through the Bo-kaap Muslim quarter of Cape Town, invited us to his home for afternoon tea and conversation; Noah, the young Zambian boy, who recited perfectly the names of all the U.S. presidents in order and then, after I gave him the agreed-upon payment of $1.00, proceeded to repeat his accomplishment, this time in reverse order. I could go on and on.

By the time we arrived in Tanzania, we were safari veterans. Joanne and I had spent several days at the Sabi Sabi game reserve on the border of Kruger National Park in South Africa and additional time at Kings Pool Camp, in a private reserve in the Linyanti area of Botswana. We had seen dozens of animal species. With fellow guests, we had climbed aboard numerous Land Rovers for morning and evening game drives, ending in traditional fashion with sundowner cocktails. Later, we had enjoyed fine candlelit dinners before retiring to our private lodges, where we slept comfortably beneath duvets in luxurious accommodations.

Our safari in Tanzania would be totally different. It was to be a ten day walking and camping trip within the Ngorongoro Conservation Area, part of the southern Serengeti Plains. Unlike the Serengeti National Park, this is a virtually tourist free area. There would be no more fancy lodges or gourmet cuisine. We would sleep in 8 foot by 10-foot tents on canvas cots with a tented hole in the ground behind for a toilet and a nearby bucket contraption for a shower. There would be no electricity. Food was abundant but less fresh with each passing day. Joining Joanne and me, was Ann, an academic from Cambridge, England who was a veteran African traveler. The safari was led by a fabled tour guide, John Stevens. He was assisted by Ched, who drove when we traveled by vehicle and by Gipson, a Maasai tribesman, whose walking stick was forever balanced by a protective rifle on his other shoulder. Our ten-person entourage was completed by four Tanzanians whose duties included erecting our tents each day prior to our late afternoon arrivals in camp, preparing meals, and heating the water for our shower buckets over a fire.

We began our ten days in the Ngorongoro Crater, the world's largest perfect caldera. This vast and diverse volcanic crater includes forest, grassland, swamps, lakes, rivers, and woodlands, and is home to thousands of zebra, wildebeest, giraffe, gazelle, buffalo, eland, warthog, lion, elephant, rhinoceros, hippopotamus, jackal, hyena, baboon, monkey, and a multitude of birds ranging from eagles to vultures. We would go on to explore the Gol Mountains and to wander through the picturesque Lake Manyara region. Our days were divided between game drives in our vehicle and exercising our legs with treks of two or three miles at a time. It was a thrill to know that usually there wasn't another tourist within 25 miles, and the only intruders at night were the lions or leopards or elephants that sometimes invaded our campsites.

The biggest pleasure for Joanne and me was our time spent on the Serengeti Plains. While Ann was an extremely knowledgeable animal lover, she wasn't much of a walker, so she would stay close to the camp or the vehicle, and Joanne and I would take off across the plains accompanied by Gipson. We would walk for miles exchanging curious glances with the zebra, wildebeest, and gazelle herds that grazed from horizon to horizon. Gipson would walk between us, his rifle ready for any encounters with lions, leopards or cheetahs. He was a striking black figure, tall and slim like most Maasai. His body was wrapped in a decorated red robe that is worn by all local male members of his tribe. Historically, the bright red was a signal of a friendly tribesman at a distance to a fellow Maasai, but today it represents pride and tradition. The Maasai were once known as terrifying warriors, but now they live peacefully, usually apart from other black or white society in Kenya or Tanzania. Their shelters are mud and dung huts which appear truly prehistoric and cattle are commonly their only significant possessions. Gipson had upset his family by leaving his village and becoming an assistant ranger and guide. His father may have been disappointed in him, but we were pleased to be in his good hands.

We made a visit to a Maasai village, a collection of a few dilapidated huts, just high enough to enter by crawling. Many of the villagers were seeing white people for the first time. They spoke no Swahili nor, of course, any English. Gipson translated our greetings into Maasai, and the males performed a ceremonial dance for us and proudly showed us their small but critical cattle herd. As implausible as it may sound, the Maasai diet consists solely of milk, blood, meat, and fat from their livestock. Fruits, vegetables and carbohydrates are completely eschewed, as is anything that lives or grows in the wild. We had been introduced to a truly remote and strange civilization. The sights, sounds, and interactions of Africa's animals filled us with constant wonder, but finding human existence so removed from our world was even more awesome.

One day in late March, well into our Tanzanian safari, Joanne, Gipson and I arrived by foot in the early afternoon at a kopje, a well-treed rocky hill, where we had a view across the plains in every direction. It would be a safe place to stop for lunch, with no danger of lions suddenly appearing. Gipson radioed to John, Ched and Ann, who were on a game drive in the vehicle. Soon they arrived with lunch, and we all secured shady spots to escape the blazing sun. It was time to rest, eat, and quench our thirsts in the 120° heat. As I always did a couple of times each day, I opened my journal, grabbed some pencils and began to write.

Shortly thereafter, Gipson asked me for my binoculars; he had spotted something in the distance. When he determined that it was a lone human being, we were incredulous for, despite all the omnipresent animals, we hadn't seen a person outside our group in days. The figure was slowly heading toward us and after nearly an hour had elapsed, it was ascertained that it was a man. As the stranger came closer to our resting place, Gipson informed us that the red robed traveler was a Maasai elder. With Gipson acting as translator, we invited him to sit down with us. He looked to be about 60, old for a Maasai, and his smile was toothless. Most incredibly, he had been walking barefoot since daybreak. He told us that he needed to visit people in each of three villages and was today traveling from one village to another. He would reach his destination by nightfall. We learned that he had three wives, numerous children, and more than 20 grandchildren. (Earlier in our safari, we had been informed about Maasai polygamous customs when Gipson told us that he was soon to marry wife number one and, a year later, he would be adding to his harem.)

The Maasai elder declined our offer of food and would not even drink our bottled water. However, he pulled from beneath the folds of his robe a jar of congealed animal fat and ate it with his fingers. We refused his invitation to sample it, and he smiled at our attempt to disguise our disgust at the concoction. The vain attempt at a food exchange had been a standoff.

We continued to talk. I was enjoying our conversation and wanted to give him something. I thought he was coveting my boots, but I needed them too much. He had been watching me write in my journal earlier, and, on a whim, I offered him one of my pencils. He took it, not knowing how to hold it. Someone in our group, perhaps Ched, produced a sheet of paper, and the old man began to scribble and then to draw in childlike fashion. He was illiterate, and he had never used a writing implement, but he enjoyed drawing on the paper. A few minutes later, the pencil had lost its edge, and I presented him with one of my 49¢ plastic pencil sharpeners and showed him how to use it. He was fascinated; to him it was a machine and unlike anything he had ever possessed.

When my new friend arose to continue his trip, he nodded good-bye to us all. Then, he smiled at me, turned to Gipson, and made a seemingly elaborate speech. Gipson said that the man wanted to express to me his sympathy to my country and its people for the disaster we had suffered last September 11th. It was a terrible thing, he said, and he hoped that nothing like it ever happens again.

I was in disbelief. How could he know anything about the World Trade Center and Pentagon bombings, I asked Gipson. My question was relayed to the Masaai elder. He told me that his villages received financial aid from the United States that allows them to survive. The Americans are good people, he said, in his language.

As he left, making his way barefoot across the plains to the distant village, I still didn't know how he had learned about the terrorism. But, I knew how this man out of another civilization felt about it, and that might be more important.

Joanne, Gipson, and Author walk the Serengeti

Epilogue

As I complete this collection of stories, Joanne and I are about to move to Mexico. It will be the fourth country in which I've lived. Might it be an environment that leads to some new stories? Perhaps, although probably not. One book is enough.

However, there are likely to be some more adventures ahead. What I have found is that I thrive on new locations and new experiences. As long as I keep moving and keep reinventing my life, it may not end. At least, that's my hope.

The warmth will be welcome. There should be some hills to climb, margaritas and music. There are sure to be clear, star-filled skies and unlimited beach. Some interesting characters, as well.

Siesta mañana.

About The Author

Ev Elting was born in New York City. He didn't stay long. He is a dual citizen of the United States and Canada and has traveled extensively through dozens of countries. He has lived in the U.S.A., Portugal, Canada, and now Mexico.

One of his achievements is the rather unusual honor of being profiled simultaneously for many years in Who's Who in America and Canadian Who's Who.

His multicultural interests are reflected in his major role in the establishment of Trinity College's innovative Human Rights Program in Hartford, Connecticut and his participation on behalf of the United Nations on its external expert Advisory Panel for the United Nations Development Report.

ISBN 141200759-3